MEN
AND THE
GODDESS

❖

Also by Tom Absher

Forms of Praise (poetry), Ohio State University Press, 1981
The Calling (poetry), Alice James Books, 1987

MEN
AND THE
GODDESS

FEMININE ARCHETYPES
IN WESTERN LITERATURE

TOM ABSHER

Park Street Press
ROCHESTER · VERMONT

Park Street Press
One Park Street
Rochester, Vermont 05767

The chapter entitled *The Epic of Gilgamesh* appeared in the fall 1988 issue
of *Anima* journal as "Gilgamesh and the Feminine."

LIBRARY OF CONGRESS CATALOGING-IN-PUBLICATION DATA

Absher, Tom, 1938–
    Men and the goddess : archetypes of the feminine in ten classics
of Western literature / Tom Absher.
        p. cm.
    Includes index.
    ISBN 0-89281-268-0
    1. Women in literature. 2. Femininity (Philosophy) in literature.
3. Archetype (Psychology) in literature. 4. Men in literature.
5. Heroes in literature. 6. Sex roles in literature. I. Title.
PN56.5.W64A27 1990
809'.89287--dc20   90-44485
                                                              CIP

Printed and bound in the United States.

10 9 8 7 6 5 4 3 2 1

Park Street Press is a division of Inner Traditions International, Ltd.

Distributed to the book trade in the United States by American International
    Distribution Corporation (AIDC)

Distributed to the book trade in Canada by Book Center, Inc., Montreal,
    Quebec

For Mark Van Doren (1894–1973) and for my three children,
Robin, Shannon, and Matthew

I believe that men also need the Goddess, and I hope they will write more about their experience.

—*Carol Christ,* Laughter of Aphrodite

When a culture begins to return to the Mother, each person in the culture begins to descend, layer after layer, into his own psyche. . . . The psychic rulers of Mycenae and Crete evidently used architecture to teach inward things—that is, they built a labyrinth.

—*Robert Bly,* Sleepers Joining Hands

Contents

Acknowledgments

Several of my colleagues at Vermont College encouraged me in the writing of this book. At different times Roy Levin, Dan Noel, and John Turner were significantly supportive. Erika Butler was especially kind in reading the entire manuscript and offering a host of editorial insights. I want to acknowledge Norwich University's generosity in granting me a sabbatical from teaching in the Adult Degree Program—a sabbatical that enabled me to write a major portion of this book. I would like to thank Barry Lane for his initial interest in the manuscript and Carol Lee Lane for her editorial assistance. Special thanks are also due to Sheila Adams for tightening the writing and to Leslie Colket who was patient and wise in guiding the book's different parts into a whole.

Preface

For over three thousand years, Western culture has been characterized by increasing male dominance and the sociopolitical, spiritual, and psychological structures of a patriarchal world view. Patriarchy brings with it, among other injustices, a literal subjugation and oppression of women and a figurative but real subjugation and disparagement of the feminine in men. In differing ways and degrees women and men are *both* victimized by the narrowly proscriptive and reductive one-sidedness of the culture of patriarchy.

Lasting works of literature reach deep into the human condition, and in so doing force an encounter with dimensions of our humanness that are lost in the process of creating a one-sided, one-dimensional, and unjust culture. Accordingly, many Western literary classics reveal not only static icons of patriarchal indoctrination but also dynamic and relevant depictions of loss. What men in particular lose by acting in culturally determined dominant roles over women, nature, and themselves is often the subject of these great works. There have been too many losses over the centuries to chronicle in a single book. In the works under examination in this book, my focus is primarily on the waste and harm male figures have experienced in devaluing and denying the feminine side of their natures.

Although no one man actually created the patriarchy, all bear responsibility for sustaining it. We cannot undo this system of dominance until we understand how it dominates and diminishes the men who run it and the women who live under it. As long as men accept male superiority as normal, they will also be forced to accept its perverting effects. In maintaining a privileged position in the patriarchy, men cooperate in an ironic subjugation of themselves.

To begin to undo the assumptions of patriarchy, men must avail themselves of feminist thought to understand patriarchy's destructive history and its destructive effects in the present. We live in an apocalyptic time, faced with not just one, but a variety of forms of global self-destruction. It is of the greatest urgency that we address these crises not only as environmentalists and politicians but also as writers, humanists, and teachers. Humans everywhere have a crucial responsibility to bring about a new consciousness.

> To know how to believe poetry and history is to know how to feel. It is also how to think, but when these two things are done deeply they are forms of the same life. We do not trust a brain without a heart, and we cannot respect a heart without a brain. It is often said, and with justice, that the contemporary world is badly educated in its feelings. (Mark Van Doren)[1]

I have dedicated this book to Mark Van Doren because as a poet, novelist, teacher, and man, he knew about the wisdom of the feminine and taught about it without ever naming it so. I was one of the fortunate students at Columbia to have studied with him. Frankly, I worshipped the man. After my father, he was the only grown man I ever loved when I was growing up. I loved him because he gave so much of himself and revealed so much of his love for books and his ways of loving the world in and through books. He was remarkably generous with his students, encouraging us to write personally, emotionally, and honestly about whatever ways books on the reading list touched or moved us. Like Plato's poet, or Poetry herself, Van Doren awakened, nourished, and strengthened the feelings in us. Robert Bly has said, "On the whole the colleges are father oriented, except for a rare teacher."[2] Mark Van Doren was such a teacher.

I'm sure he was as flawed as the next man, but what I saw in class was a man aspiring to be a whole person and revealing his life to us as he did so. I remember him saying, "There is nothing more disgusting than a completely masculine man or a completely feminine woman. There is something of both sexes in us; something of the child too."[3] To my sophomore self in 1959, a self that had grown up in Texas, this was a radical view. Because Van Doren was such a distinguished professor and a Pulitzer Prize-winning poet, one couldn't very well disparage him as being *less* of a man for such a remark. Clearly he was more a man, more human for the way he went about acknowledging and incorporating the elements of the feminine in himself. Van Doren's classes were my first real introduction to the notion that men had a feminine side and that one way of experiencing that side was through reading and writing about great works of literature. He encouraged reading and writing with a nonproscriptive approach to feelings.

I went on to become a teacher of literature, and in the early 1970s I began to write poetry and practice meditation. I discovered that these activities were further ways of experiencing the sacred feminine in myself. The work of Robert Bly began to be a major influence in my life around that time because he has written and said a great deal about the importance of the sacred feminine in men's lives, whether they are poets or not. Bly also expressly discussed meditation (in any form) as one way men have of encountering the feminine spirit within.

The great works of Western literature often depict a centuries-old tragic cost of male egocentricity and reveal insights that can bring about constructive change. The stories of Gilgamesh, Willy Loman, Odysseus, Huck Finn, Macbeth, Bottom, Sir Gawain, Ivan Ilyich, Ike McCaslin, and Mr. Ramsay demonstrate two kinds of male brotherhood. They show the brotherhood of pain that results from the impairment men experience when they suppress aspects of the sacred feminine in the world in themselves and the brotherhood of healing that can only occur when men begin to live in harmony with the feminine. Like Daedalus, the great architect and inventor of Greek mythology, men have designed and built the very labyrinth that now traps them. If men can muster the courage necessary for personal change and reinvention of the self, we may yet be able to discover the way out.

[1] Mark Van Doren, *Liberal Education* (Boston: Beacon Hill, 1962), p. 162.

[2] Robert Bly, *Talking All Morning* (Ann Arbor, MI: University of Michigan Press, 1980), p. 214.

[3] It was March 2, 1959, Comp. Lit. 244. I still have all my notes from his classes.

Introduction

I have great sympathy for the general feminine principle in life.
I find very little "heroic" about most men, and . . . that ours is in
general a heroic age seems to me ridiculous. We are near stifling
and exterminating our planet. . . . In terms of history men have
failed; it is time we tried Eve.

—*John Fowles*

When we acknowledge that Eve is one of many metaphoric daughters
of the Goddess, then clearly her time has come. The Goddess is returning in many different forms, profoundly influencing the lives and consciousness of many people. What this will mean is as far ranging and
complex as the growing literature on the subject. The Goddess is being
rediscovered in archaeology, mythology, folklore, psychology, spirituality, art, literature, and ecology—just to form a partial list.[1] In the
foreword to Marija Gimbutas' *The Language of the Goddess,* her second major study of the prehistoric archaeology of the Goddess, Joseph
Campbell writes, "One cannot but feel that in the appearance of this
volume at just this turn of the century there is an evident relevance to
the universally recognized need in our time for a general transformation of consciousness."[2]

The Goddess, in Merlin Stone's terms, is the "divine feminine principle" or the "sacred feminine principle in the universe."[3] It is this
principle that is desperately needed in the world today. It is needed by
all of us, men and women.

Novelist and scholar Marilyn French writes in her book,
Shakespeare's Division of Experience:

For Westerners of the twentieth century, it is the masculine principle
and its total dedication to power and control in every area of existence

1

that threatens to extinguish not only human felicity but the human race itself. . . . Western culture is founded on misogyny because the urge to power requires devaluing those things it seeks power over, and those things have traditionally been associated with women. The way out of the bind—and it is a bind—the way to alter the world's suicidal course, seems to me to be to abandon these divisions, to see all of human experience as good and available to all humans.[4]

Her argument throughout her study of the plays is that while Shakespeare began his career with great respect for masculine qualities and some suspicion of feminine ones, in his later works "He had come to fear and deplore the power and capriciousness of the masculine principle and to idealize certain aspects of the feminine."[5] If it seems that in this book I too share this bias toward the feminine, it is not because I deplore the masculine principle but because I think we need to *emphasize* the importance of the feminine in order to restore the balance between the two. In *The Chalice and the Blade,* Riane Eisler speaks of "a partnership society where men and women (and 'masculine' and 'feminine') are accorded equal value."[6] The problem is that for too long the masculine principle has been allowed to function alone, separate from the balancing powers of the feminine. It would be equally unbalanced if the situation had been reversed and the feminine principle were operating apart from the masculine. Ann Ulanov writes, "The feminine is half of human wholeness, an essential part of it, without which wholeness is impossible. . . . [But] wholeness means both poles, both modes, and wholeness is not simply identification and fusion but polarity and union."[7]

For thousands of years, patriarchy has gradually increased its emphasis on the masculine principle as it increased its dominance over women, nature, and "all that has been considered female,"[8] including the feminine principle in both men and in women. Gerda Lerner states in her conclusion to *The Creation of Patriarchy:*

By making the term "man" subsume "woman" and arrogate to itself the representation of all of humanity, men have built a conceptual error of vast proportion into all of their thought. By taking the half for the whole, they have not only missed the essence of whatever they are describing, but they have distorted it in such a fashion that they

cannot see it correctly. . . . The androcentric fallacy, which is built
into all the mental constructs of Western civilization, cannot be
rectified by "adding women." What it demands for rectification is a
radical restructuring of thought and analysis which once and for all
accepts the fact that humanity consists in equal parts of men and
women.[9]

In part, this "radical restructuring of thought and analysis" involves the
return of the Goddess, the return of the sacred feminine principle in the
consciousness and lives of men and women.

The genesis of this book dates from the early days of my college
teaching career. I had begun to work some of the classics of Western
literature into my classes. It was the early seventies, the early days of
feminism. Around that time a woman said to me that she had decided
against studying the classics because they were primarily written by
men, were mostly about men, and that finally, in her view, they sup-
ported the status quo of the male-dominated culture. It was a sweeping
generalization, but I took it to heart and thought about it over a number
of years as I read for and taught my classes. What I began to discover
was that while many of the male figures in these works often do mirror
the male-dominated culture and its values, those values are often the
heart of the characters' problems. Men like Gilgamesh, Macbeth, Ivan
Ilyich, and Willy Loman have *suffered* from the great imbalances of
patriarchal culture; their stories reflect the tragic effects of this imbalance, a fundamental lack of the mythic feminine.

In the many books and essays on the Goddess, women have led the
resurgence of the mythic feminine as a force of consciousness. A number of these works stress, appropriately, the specific value of the Goddess to women, but men have a great need for the mythic feminine as
well. In fact, men *and* women are both accountable for constructing and
sustaining the imbalances of patriarchal consciousness and are victimized by it. Ironically, men may indeed have the more urgent need for
the Goddess if they are ever to find ways of restoring balance to their
thinking and their lives. The importance of the feminine in male consciousness has been present from the very beginnings of patriarchy. I
believe that this feminine mode of thought and being may be experienced
and studied through many of the classics in Western literature, and that

this feminine wisdom has been with us all along in our literature. It is *we* who have gradually grown blind to it.

As early as Plato's time we can see the groundwork being laid for a vision of society and ways of being that specifically exclude the feminine. In Book Ten of *The Republic*, Plato, using the persona of Socrates, says: "We shall be right in refusing to admit him [the poet] into a well-ordered State, because he awakens and nourishes and strengthens the feelings and impairs the reason. . . . he is a manufacturer of images and is very far removed from truth."[10] Later, speaking of poetry itself as a "she," Plato explains that "poetry feeds and waters the passions instead of drying them up; she lets them rule, although they ought to be controlled. . . . we must remain firm in our conviction that hymns to the *gods* and praises of famous *men* are the only poetry which ought to be admitted into our State."[11]

We are a long way from Plato's Athens and the fifth century B.C.E., but many men today will recognize this vision of culture as being not unlike the one they've experienced. In a collection of interviews called *Talking All Morning,* contemporary poet Robert Bly sees the American version of the patriarchy in striking terms:

> The whole drive of American culture is toward a sort of brutal masculinity. . . . The American culture teaches the male to crush and suppress the woman inside of him. What we see in the typical football player is a man who has crushed everything feminine in him and has allowed only the masculine to live. He mistreats women, because he has always mistreated the woman that is inside him. Once he has crushed the feminine part of himself, he becomes unstable.[12]

One of the terrible paradoxes for men brought up in a patriarchal culture is that we have been taught not to feel and not to express what we feel, and we lose touch with how we too have been wounded by an imbalanced culture. When our inner emotional lives are diminished or even extinguished, our humanity is foreshortened. Often we don't realize it because our learned denial dominates, suppressing even our own pain. Stoicism replaces ways of experiencing pain with numbness. We deny not only our own pain but empathy with the pain of others and the very pain of the Earth.

Marilyn French points out that as long as Shakespeare's King Lear is *nothing else* but King, he is not fully human. However, when in the play he abandons the masculine principle's power, privilege, hierarchy, and reason, he loses his "shield against the human."[13] King Lear's fall from power into pain and suffering "does not strip him of his manhood, it confers humanhood upon him."[14] King Lear loses his kingship, but gains his humanity. He learns to "see feelingly,"[15] which is the wisdom of the feminine, a wisdom men by and large are *not* taught in a male-dominated culture.

The encounter with the feminine in these ten classic stories shows men facing or being faced with the fact of their own woundedness at the hands of the patriarchy and the dehumanizing effects of their denial of their feminine selves. In an interview between Bly and Ekbert Fass in *Talking All Morning,* Bly makes the observation: "What the Grail poems discuss even more is some strange creature who is wounded. He has a bit of steel or iron in his testicles, and he can't be healed; this wound remains unhealed century after century. So there is such a thing as 'wound literature.' . . .in our time the wound is beginning to live and be lived again."[16] Fass, the interviewer, responds: "'The Waste Land' brings it up. . . .Ted Hughes [the English poet] once described the poem to me as a love poem for this degraded and desecrated female spirit." Bly agrees and offers the judgment that "now no work is of any value that does not face the wound."[17] I think that there are, in fact, many examples of this wound literature in the canon of Western literature and that when we read and experience them with this perspective, they can help us to face the wound and to even begin the healing process.

Throughout these great stories, we see the regenerative figure of the Green Man in one metaphoric form or another. In his book *Witchcraft in the Middle Ages,* Jeffrey Burton Russell describes the Green Man as "witches' familiars . . . fertility spirits . . . any of whom could be either frightening or funny . . . Robin Hood may have originally been a Green Man and his hood not an article of clothing but a bull's head or half."[18] Russell says that Robin Goodfellow was such a spirit, and that these spirits:

> could take the form of animals or of little men or render themselves
> invisible. . . . This variation of shape was perfectly acceptable to a
> world view in which apart from the animal world there was a real,
> spiritual world where a man and an animal—or God and a piece of
> bread—could have the same essence.[19]

The Green Man is an archetype for an androgynous, regenerative spirit connected with the earth and its vegetation about which relatively little has been written. In the notes to his long poem by the same name, Ronald Johnson writes:

> The Green Man of the title is not a poetic metaphor, merely, but is still to be seen in England. It is not uncommon for pubs or inns to be called by his name, a holdover from times when he was a current legend and was deeply associated with Robin Hood and the Green Knight in *Gawain and the Green Knight*. . . . As King of the May, or Jack-in-the-Green, he has a persistent history that can be traced back to May Day celebrations throughout Northern and Central Europe.[20]

This archetype appears again and again as a striking contrast to the cultural mandate of perfection, often utilizing the easygoing laughter of regenerative naturalness. In these works, the archetype underscores the tension between masculine and feminine ways of knowing and being— the former characterized by single-mindedness and rigid control, and the later by expansiveness and acceptance.

[1] See Bibliography at the end of the book.

[2] Joseph Campbell, "Foreword," Marija Gimbutas, *The Language of the Goddess* (New York: Harper & Row, 1989), p. xiv.

[3] Merlin Stone, "Introduction," *The Goddess Re-Awakening*, ed. Shirley Nicholson (Wheaton: Theosophical Publishing House, 1989), pp. 4–5.

[4] Marilyn French, *Shakespeare's Division of Experience* (London: Jonathan Cape, 1982), pp. 340–1.

[5] *Ibid.*, p. 17.

[6] Riane Eisler, *The Chalice and the Blade* (New York: Harper & Row, 1987), p. 206, note 10.

[7] Ann Belford Ulanov, *The Feminine in Jungian Psychology and in Christian Theology* (Evanston, IL: Northwestern University Press, 1971), pp. 156–57.

[8] Char McKee, "Feminism: A Vision of Love," *The Goddess Re-Awakening*, p. 265.

[9] Gerda Lerner, *The Creation of Patriarchy* (New York: Oxford University Press, 1986), p. 220.

[10] *The Portable Plato*, translated by Benjamin Jowett (New York: Viking, 1965), p. 674.

[11] *Ibid.*, p. 676. Italics mine.

[12] Robert Bly, *Talking All Morning* (Ann Arbor, MI: University of Michigan Press, 1980), pp. 66–67.

[13] French, op. cit., p. 223.

[14] *Ibid.*, p. 222–23.

[15] In *King Lear* this phrase is spoken by Gloucester (IV.vi. 146), but is the motto for Lear himself as well by the play's end.

[16] Bly, op. cit., p. 273.

[17] *Ibid.*, p. 273.

[18] Jeffrey Burton Russell, *Witchcraft in the Middle Ages* (Ithaca, NY: Cornell University Press, 1972), p. 52.

[19] *Ibid.*, p. 53.

[20] Ronald Johnson, *The Book of the Green Man: A Poem* (New York: W.W. Norton, 1967), notes, p. 89.

1

The Epic of Gilgamesh

The Great Goddess, rather unlike the great male gods, is multidimensional. *Gilgamesh* depicts that polymorphous and sometimes contradictory nature in a great variety of ways.

—*John Gardner and John Maier*

This relatively short epic was discovered written on clay tablets in Iraq in the last century. It dates from roughly 3,000 B.C.E. and is widely regarded as the oldest work of Western literature. It tells the story of Gilgamesh, an arrogant, selfish King of Uruk who sexually violates every bride in his kingdom on her wedding night. The people of Uruk are outraged and call on the goddesses to morally regenerate him. These divine female figures initiate the process by creating Enkidu, a wild man from the forest, whom Gilgamesh comes to cherish as a friend. They have many adventures together. When Enkidu dies, Gilgamesh is bereft and frightened of his own death. He goes on a long journey to seek immortality. It is denied him, and he is confronted with experiences that consistently remind him of his mortality. When he dies, he feels his life has been a failure even though he has started to become an emotionally sound and compassionate human being.

The Epic of Gilgamesh is the story of one man's moral regeneration and spiritual education through his struggles and contacts with the divine feminine in all its personifications and its wisdom. In spite of his physical perfection, great beauty, and courage, Gilgamesh, the King of Uruk, is fundamentally arrogant and selfish at the outset of the narrative. Gilgamesh is two-thirds god and one-third human, but to his people and the gods he is morally blind. That blindness is primarily expressed as sexual oppression of women. "His arrogance has no bounds by day or night. . . . His lust leaves no virgin to her lover, neither the warrior's daughter nor the wife of the noble."[1] In practice this means Gilgamesh sleeps with every bride in his kingdom on her wedding night. Because it is his lust rather than custom that motivates him, he is an interloper in the marriage bed who violates both the bride and the bridegroom. The people of Uruk are disturbed and angry. They lament to the goddesses, demanding that Gilgamesh confront his double: "Create his equal; let it be as like him as his own reflection, his second self, stormy heart for stormy heart. Let them contend together and leave Uruk in quiet" (p. 62). They ask that their king be made to see himself and overcome his selfishness through contact with his own reflection. He must overcome his arrogance through self-awareness and self-struggle.

Gilgamesh reveals himself to be devoid of empathy and a moral sense of his responsibility for right action in the lives of others. Moreover, he allows his lust to violate the principle of marriage, the *hierosgamos,* a sacred union of opposites. This demonstrates how far he is from inner wholeness and harmony. In her book, *Descent to the Goddess, A Way of Initiation for Women,* Sylvia Perera explores the journey of the goddess Inanna-Ishtar to the underworld for renewal. The story of Gilgamesh can be seen as the male version of this journey and renewal. Perera might well be speaking of Gilgamesh when she notes "The reactions of the narcissistic man who negates or belittles his partner's pain. . . . Thus he betrays his need to descend into the underworld himself, his need to find a relationship to an inner feminine whom he can accept nondefensively and revere as equal."[2] This is precisely what the goddesses prepare for Gilgamesh in the figure of Enkidu. He is a male embodiment of certain parts of the feminine, the anima that Gilgamesh knows nothing about.

Before meeting Enkidu, Gilgamesh is depicted as solitary, aggressive, sexually self-aggrandizing, and "like a wild bull . . . lord[ing] it over men" (p. 65). It is disturbingly ironic that the earliest known work of Western literature opens with a characterization of a protagonist still popular in many of our male heroes. Unlike the people of Uruk, we are not demanding from our goddesses a modifying figure to bring about change in those male figures.

Aruru, the "mother goddess"[3] who created Gilgamesh, now creates Enkidu. He is given all the strength and manliness that he needs to be Gilgamesh's equal (although Gilgamesh will outdo him in their contest of strength). Enkidu also has what Gilgamesh lacks, a fully developed *anima*, or feminine side. Enkidu has "long hair like a woman's, it waved like the hair of Nisaba, the goddess of corn" (p. 63). More important, Enkidu ". . . longed for a comrade, for one who would understand his heart" (p. 65). In moral terms Enkidu represents emotionality, feelings, companionship, and an awareness of otherness for Gilgamesh.

Before he meets Gilgamesh, Enkidu is depicted as a wild man completely identified with nature: "Enkidu ate grass in the hills with the gazelle and lurked with wild beasts at the water-hole; he had joy of the water with the herds of wild game" (p. 63). This association of Enkidu with wildness and animals strengthens his role as the first (but not the last) bringer of feminine wisdom to Gilgamesh. Nature and animals have long been regarded as a source and home of the feminine, the Great Goddess.[4] In all of his aspects Enkidu represents probably the oldest portrayal of the archetype of the Green Man.

As further preparation for his meeting with Gilgamesh, Enkidu is trained in the art of love by a temple prostitute, called a "love-priestess" in another translation.[5] After six days and seven nights of lovemaking with her, Enkidu learns "the woman's art" (p. 64). There is an enormous contrast between this kind of mutually satisfying lovemaking and Gilgamesh's narcissistic *de facto* rapes, which have in them none of a woman's feelings, much less her "art."

Before he meets Enkidu, Gilgamesh dreams of finding a star that has just fallen from heaven. He tries to lift it, but it is too heavy. He tells his mother, Ninsun, one of the wise deities, about the dream.[6] To him "its attraction was like the love of woman" (p. 66). Ninsun explains that "this star of heaven . . . is the strong comrade, the one who brings help to his friend in need. He is the strongest of the wild creatures, the stuff of Anu; born in the grass-lands and the wild hills reared him; when you see him you will be glad; you will love him as a woman and he will never forsake you. This is the meaning of the dream" (p. 66). In Gardner and Maier's translation, Ninsun tells Gilgamesh that he will "hug" and "love" Enkidu "like a wife."[7]

The one who comes to teach Gilgamesh is seen as both a star of heaven and a wild creature reared by the hills. Enkidu is a creature of both heaven and earth. His greater wholeness and authority (although we will see that he is not perfectly whole or without flaws) help to shake Gilgamesh out of narrow, selfish one-sidedness. Enkidu is the driving force behind Gilgamesh's voyage into the underworld. Because Enkidu is from the heavens, the earth, and the underworld, he is clearly a Green Man who is an emissary of the divine feminine. As Sylvia Perera observes, "Already in ancient Sumer . . . the Great Goddess had been split in various ways, including into upper and lower world aspects. Thus there was a necessity to traverse both regions to restore a sense of creative wholeness and to comprehend the rhythmic interplay of life. Inanna, Queen of Heaven, was perhaps the first initiate described in writing to suffer this journey."[8] If Inanna is the first initiate, Gilgamesh may well be the second. His journey is taken in behalf of Enkidu, who declares, "I have come to change the old order" (p. 65).

The woman who instructs Enkidu in lovemaking now makes final preparations for Enkidu's meeting with Gilgamesh by showing him how to eat bread and drink wine. She also dresses him in her clothing. "She divided her clothing in two and with the one half she clothed him and the other herself; and holding his hand she led him like a child to the sheepfolds, into the shepherds' tents" (p. 67).[9] At this point, Enkidu is completely identified with feminine power. Not only his reason for being, his birth, his instruction, and preparation for meeting Gilgamesh, but also everything in the story thus far shows the divine feminine, in the form of Sumerian goddesses, overseeing the restoration of just order. Gilgamesh's psychic order and the subsequent order of the society he rules are also to be set right by the intervention of the divine feminine.

On a night when Gilgamesh once again sets out "to be first with the bride" (p. 68), Enkidu goes to meet him at "the place where Gilgamesh lords it over the people" (p. 68) and steps forward, blocking Gilgamesh's way. Like two bulls they wrestle, and Enkidu is thrown. Enkidu praises Gilgamesh's strength, and immediately they embrace "and their friendship was sealed" (p. 69).

The first adventure of Enkidu and Gilgamesh is a journey into the forest to hunt down and kill the "monster" Humbaba. Gilgamesh has a prophetic dream about his destiny, and Enkidu interprets it for him. Throughout *The Epic of Gilgamesh,* whenever Gilgamesh dreams, others interpret it for him. His mother explains the first dream, and Enkidu interprets all the others. Gilgamesh is not familiar enough with his unconscious and must turn to others whose deep association with the sacred feminine gives that familiarity and insight.

Enkidu explains to Gilgamesh that the dream is about his destiny.

> The meaning of the dream is this. The father of the gods has given
> you kingship, such is your destiny, everlasting life is not your destiny.
> Because of this do not be sad at heart, do not be grieved or oppressed.
> He has given you power to bind and to loose, to be the darkness and
> the light of mankind. . . . But do not abuse this power, deal justly with
> your servants in the palace, deal justly before Shamash. (p. 70)

In the dream and its interpretation, Gilgamesh is presented with a paradoxical wisdom he will meet repeatedly. His central struggle will be to comprehend it throughout the rest of the narrative. It is paradoxical because it points not to a single fixed, monolithic axiom of truth, but to moral human powers involving a process of reconciling opposites. Erich Neumann defines such wisdom as feminine or "matriarchal" and says that it is "the wisdom of the unconscious, of the instincts, of life, and of relationship. . . .Matriarchal wisdom is paradoxical. It never separates and juxtaposes opposites with the clear discrimination of patriarchal consciousness; rather, it relates them to one another by an 'as well as' or an 'also.'"[10]

Enkidu's statement of the paradoxical power "to bind and to loose" is found in two other relevant places. In the Gospel According to Matthew, Christ says on two occasions (once to Peter and once to the assembled disciples) "Whatsoever ye shall bind on earth shall be bound in heaven; and whatsoever ye shall loose on earth shall be loosed in heaven."[11] Carl Jung writes in *Aspects of the Feminine*: "Woman's psychology is founded on the principle of Eros, the great binder and loosener."[12] This points strongly to the give and take, the process of forbidding and allowing, in the dynamic of human exchange that is characteristic of "just" relationships. At the beginning of the story Gilgamesh is in extreme narcissistic isolation. He then meets his double, his larger, more feminine self as Enkidu. Enkidu interprets his dream as a dream that points toward moral relationships with others and toward change. Everlasting life, which by denying death would be a form of stasis, is not to be Gilgamesh's fate, regardless of how much he might wish it.

Sylvia Perera asserts that there is a part of all of us that is frightened and disgusted with change and, like Gilgamesh, wants eternity and stasis. "But as the goddess is also matter, there is no stasis and no eternity of form possible for material life. . . . We must go beyond Gilgamesh's and the patriarchal ego's denigration of the goddess as fickle and learn to serve her rather as inconstant. This is the primary psychological task to which our age is called."[13]

What Gilgamesh does not yet understand and what he perhaps never fully understands is that the power to bind and to loose and to be the darkness and the light are in fact great mortal powers stemming from the feminine. But Gilgamesh is learning. When he and Enkidu finally do encounter the giant Humbaba, the giant is really quite gentle and humble, and Gilgamesh is moved by his gestures of friendliness and offers of servitude.

> The tears started to his eyes and he was pale. . . . 'Let me go free, Gilgamesh, and I will be your servant, you shall be my lord; all the trees of the forest that I tended on the mountain shall be yours. I will cut them down and build you a palace.' He took him by the hand and led him to his house, so that the heart of Gilgamesh was moved with compassion. Gilgamesh swore by the heavenly life, by the earthly life, by the underworld itself: 'O Enkidu, should not the snared bird return to its nest, the captive man return to his mother's arms?' (p. 82)

Given the selfish, blind arrogance of Gilgamesh at the outset of the narrative, this response reveals a substantial change on his part toward developing compassion and empathy. The giant offers to build Gilgamesh a palace and takes Gilgamesh by the hand and leads him to his house. Like Enkidu, who is a creature connected to the heavens, the earth, and the underworld, Gilgamesh swears by these three interconnected realms and shows empathy in his reference to returning the snared bird to its nest and the captive man to his mother's arms. This underscores emergence of a sensitive, emotive capacity of the feminine power within him. Gilgamesh has come a long way from violating young women on their wedding night. But he has not yet come far enough, for he gives in to Enkidu's insistence that Humbaba must die. Together they kill "the guardian of the forest" (p. 83).

In an overall view of the story this is an error. Gilgamesh and Enkidu have made a long, hard journey into the forest, locus of the feminine; in the encounter with Humbaba, Gilgamesh's compassion is awakened. But when they kill the giant, the essence of this adventure seems violated to me. Enkidu insists that they stick to their plan to kill the giant; and, as a result, the gods are angered and ultimately take Enkidu's life. In theory, Humbaba is a terrible giant who must be killed; in fact, when they encounter him in the flesh, he is all noise and bluster; then, gentle and kind. In this sense, Humbaba, too, is a paradox. Gilgamesh and Enkidu are not able to change their behavior and their plan accordingly. Rather than acknowledge what they know in their hearts about the giant, they stick to their original plan and kill him. Humbaba is killed, then, because their orderly, patriarchal sense of duty and rational consistency overrides their intuitive perception of the inconsistent, experiential present. As Gilgamesh said before embarking on the adventure, "I am committed to this enterprise: to climb the mountain, to cut down the cedar, and to leave behind me an enduring name" (p. 73). So underlying it all is Gilgamesh's pursuit of fame and immortality. A similarly willful, dogged determination to win fame leads to Achilles' personal tragedy in *The Iliad*.

Gilgamesh and Enkidu slay the guardian of the forest, and in response Nature itself is thrown into confusion: "Now the mountains were moved and all the hills, for the guardian of the forest was killed" (p. 83). Enil, god of earth and wind, is enraged at the beheading of Humbaba, but it will take one more act of foolish pride before Gilgamesh is punished.

In his second act of hubris, Gilgamesh rudely and insultingly refuses the sexual advances and marriage proposal of the great Sumerian goddess Ishtar. Ironically, he rejects her on the grounds of her reputation for inconstancy—this from a man whose very story begins with the account of his violation of all the young brides in his kingdom. The tables are turned. Now that Gilgamesh is on the receiving end of inconstancy rather than the initiator of it, he has a new awareness of the experience. "And if you and I should be lovers, should not I be served in the same fashion as all these others who you loved once?" (p. 87). This question with its implied rejection greatly enrages Ishtar and precipitates Enkidu's death, but at this point it also reflects how much Gilgamesh has changed. The man who made a personal institution of "one-night stands" now respects and desires constancy, but it is not enough.

Gilgamesh and Enkidu are still full of their recent killing. When Ishtar sends the Bull of Heaven down to them, they destroy it. Enkidu even tears out its right thigh and tosses it in the face of the goddess Ishtar. For this act of great impiety, Ishtar curses Enkidu with a fatal sickness.

What kind of example or tutor in the ways of the feminine is Enkidu if his own actions lead to the death of the guardian of the forest and insulting behavior to Ishtar? Since the feminine is a whole constellation of ways of knowing and being, attitudes and insights, no one human possesses all of it; no man or woman ever masters the feminine. Enkidu came to Gilgamesh so that the king might *begin* his education. Gilgamesh needs to understand what Erich Neumann calls "matriarchal consciousness," or the deep "center of consciousness in the heart."[14] Enkidu thus turns Gilgamesh from his heartless sexual exploitation of women and opens Gilgamesh's heart through their friendship. By the time Enkidu is on his deathbed, their bond is depicted as a deep emotional brotherhood. The process of struggle and conflict progresses to a gradual openness as Gilgamesh turns from the received code of his arrogant, militant maleness toward a more humble, emotional series of encounters with the sacred feminine. *The Epic of Gilgamesh* teaches us that while others may assist us in these encounters, ultimately men must descend into the center of their psyche and encounter the nascent power of the sacred feminine alone. It is the lesson Odysseus learns on his voyage home alone; Huck learns it lighting out for the Territory ahead of the others; and Ike McCaslin discovers it when he enters the wilderness alone and unarmed.

When Enkidu dies, Gilgamesh is distraught and bereft. His emotionality reflects how far removed he is from his former selfishness and arrogance. There is an ironic reference to Gilgamesh's former victims as he veils Enkidu, "When Gilgamesh touched [Enkidu's] heart, it did not beat. So Gilgamesh laid a veil, as one veils the bride, over his friend.

He began to rage like a lion, like a lioness robbed of her whelp. This way and that he paced round the bed; he tore out his hair and strewed it around. He dragged off his splendid robes and flung them down as though they were abominations" (p. 95). Gilgamesh is naked and alone in his grief and distress. This has been Enkidu's work. In life he opened Gilgamesh's heart and the unconscious world of his dreams; in death he leads Gilgamesh deeper into his unconscious. Enkidu's creation by Anu, his long hair, and his several characterizations as "bride," and "lover" indicate that he is clearly Gilgamesh's psychopomp, a divine messenger created to be Gilgamesh's spirit guide into the underworld. Enkidu leads Gilgamesh out of his solitary, emotionally insulated, sexually exploitative, arrogant, patriarchal self toward becoming a vulnerable, loving, grieving, angry, and emotional friend. Through the divine agency of Enkidu, Gilgamesh will become profoundly initiated into the feminine realm of the heart and be able to express emotional relatedness to others. In Martin Buber's terms, Gilgamesh will move from a soul-deadening, dehumanizing, egocentric I-It consciousness toward the experience of an I-Thou human relationship.[15] Gilgamesh, the legendary and possibly historical builder of "the walls of Uruk," begins now to take down some of his own walls. If Enkidu was Gilgamesh's Thou, with Enkidu's death Gilgamesh descends to discover his own inner Thou as he struggles to come to terms with Enkidu's death and his own mortality. In *Religion and the Unconscious,* Ann and Barry Ulanov write, "The worlds of consciousness and the unconscious . . . are mirrored in the network of psychic connections between self and other. To be a person means to be both conscious and unconscious. The more related these are, the more a person one is . . . the self needs an other to become a self."[16] Gilgamesh who once wounded others is now the wounded one and is becoming a fuller person because of his suffering.

Fearing his own death and grieving for Enkidu, Gilgamesh begins his arduous supernatural journey into the underworld. He hopes to learn from Utnapishtim, who was granted everlasting life by the gods, the secret of immortality. Gilgamesh journeys past the Man-Scorpions, through the mountain of Mashu and its twelve leagues of darkness, into the garden of the gods where the bushes bear fruits of carnelian, lapis lazuli, agate, and pearls. Gilgamesh wears animal skins and has " . . . a face like the face of one who has made a long journey" (p. 100). He tells Siduri, a woman winemaker he encounters, "Enkidu my brother, whom I loved, the end of mortality has overtaken him. I wept for him seven days and nights till the worm fastened on him. Because of my brother I am afraid of death, because of my brother I stray through the wilderness and cannot rest" (p. 101). Siduri, whom Joseph Campbell calls "a manifestation of the Goddess Ishtar,"[17] counsels him to accept his mortality and to see it for all that is good about it. She points out that the time spent in a futile pursuit of immortality is time spent away from the sweet pleasures of mortality, of life lived in the moment. Gilgamesh is creating his own pain by searching for immortal life when he could be enjoying mortal life.

Throughout the narrative Gilgamesh has been aided, counseled, and instructed in the feminine primarily by women. Siduri's advice is no exception. The quest for immortality is really a male or patriarchal approach to time. Gilgamesh wants to master, to dominate time, and thereby live forever. The wisdom Siduri offers focuses on the quality of time rather than its quantity. Siduri's point is that in living for some grandiose future goal like gaining eternal life, Gilgamesh is not alive to the present. This patriarchal orientation to existence is prevalent in many male figures in literature; Gilgamesh is not unlike Achilles, Macbeth, or Willie Loman in his view of time. Against this vision of time as a quantified chronology with a future orientation, Siduri offers wise words of counsel based in the feminine: "As for you, Gilgamesh, fill your belly with good things; day and night, night and day, dance and be merry, feast and rejoice. Let your clothes be fresh, bathe yourself in water, cherish the little child that holds your hand, and make your wife happy in your embrace; for this, too, is the lot of man" (p. 102).

This way of viewing time is crucial to an understanding of the nature of the sacred feminine, for as Ann Belford Ulanov says, "The feminine sense of time is always of the moment; it is not chronos, but kairos."[18] If we don't know how to live in the moment, to grasp and savor the finite now, just as it is, what difference will it make if we have an infinite number of moments? Immortal life would only be a longer series of unappreciated moments. If we don't know how to value a finite series of breaths and waking days, having an infinite series at our disposal will only prolong our ignorance and our abuse of time. Immortal life would be wasted on us. Gilgamesh, who really seems most interested in immortality as a self-aggrandizing extension of his ego, is actually least suited for it. With her deep, appreciation of life and its sweet, ordinary moments, Siduri knows best how to live forever!

Gilgamesh doesn't heed Siduri's counsel; he sets out to meet Utnapishtim. When he does finally meet the one called "the Faraway," it is Utnapishtim's wife—another woman who assists Gilgamesh on his journey. She urges her husband to tell Gilgamesh of the secret plant, "a mystery of the gods . . . that grows under the water, it has a prickle like a thorn, like a rose; it will wound your hands, but if you succeed in taking it, then your hands will hold that which restores his lost youth to a man" (p. 116).

Gilgamesh then makes his journey in the underworld where the plant grows, descending to the bottom of what Campbell calls the "cosmic sea," and retrieves it.[19] In a poignant moment of inattention (Gilgamesh is *not* attuned to living in the moment) "a serpent . . . sensed the sweetness of the flower . . . and snatched it away and immediately . . . sloughed its skin . . . ." (p. 117). After eating the plant, the serpent sheds its skin and symbolically gains the immortality Gilgamesh thought was his.[20] Gilgamesh weeps, saying, "For myself I have gained nothing; not I, but the beast of the earth has joy of it now. . . . I found a sign and now I have lost it" (p. 117).

Gilgamesh returns home to Uruk and dies shortly thereafter. Tragically, for all his education in and experience of the feminine, he still sees his life more in terms of its failed achievements than its divine insights and revelations. To have been given a sign, to have made contact with the secret of divine immortality, is, for Gilgamesh, seen in egocentric, materialistic terms: "For *myself I have gained* nothing . . . ." (p. 117; italics mine). Gilgamesh wants the rose as a trophy of immortality; his revelations and epiphanies will not suffice. It is this failure of his gratitude, his materialistic selfishness, that precipitates the ironic loss of the gift. Gilgamesh is full of himself and his reputation; the ultimate measure of the divine would be wasted on him. In the last section of the story, the narrator offers Gilgamesh consolation and advice in the same words Enkidu used earlier in the story: "O Gilgamesh, this was the meaning of your dream. You were given the kingship, such was your destiny, everlasting life was not your destiny. Because of this do not be sad at heart, do not be grieved or oppressed; . . . [you were] given . . . power to bind and to loose, to be the darkness and the light of mankind" (p. 118).

The Gilgamesh who dies at the end of the epic is greatly changed from the totally selfish despot who opened it. He is, however, appropriately still not whole or perfect. It gives the narrative a base of realism in spite of all its supernatural events. Gilgamesh has developed and grown but remains true to his character. It is to the epic's credit as literature that there is much magic in the story, but no magical human reversals.

Men and women alike are victims of the dominant culture and its patriarchal consciousness. We are all more or less disposed to want the visible, material trophies of accomplishment. We seek the things that can win the applause of others rather than the invisible, spiritual signs of divine revelation. To most of us, signs are useless and gather us no praise from others. We hold public prizes and trophies in high esteem and do not value epiphanies and the knowledge of spiritual paradoxes. Gilgamesh dies after what he considers a futile search for the prize. Five millennia later, we may come to relish the life that comes from choosing the moment. The final paradox of Gilgamesh is that while the hero thought his life a failure because he didn't obtain the rose of immortality, the story itself (a story of *mortal* humanity) may well be immortal.

Personal Commentary

It is uncanny that such an ancient literary work as *The Epic of Gilgamesh* can be so immediately relevant to the kind of imbalances I feel in myself and see in the male-dominated culture around me. I have no trouble identifying with Gilgamesh. His inherent male arrogance, his assumptions of exploitative sexuality, his obsession with immortality, and the tangible objectification of fame are all part of the baggage of a male ego. It is like being one with a great, destructive brotherhood.

It disturbs and depresses me to identify with a man from 3,000 B.C.E. in this way, for it reveals the tenacity of male-dominated values and an inability to change. Then I see myself and some of the men around me who are trying to change. I am heartened that there are younger men who simply do not accept the old patriarchal assumptions as givens. The book heartens me, too, because it is about change. Gilgamesh does make enormous changes by the end of his life. He begins to regain his heart, soul, and feelings; he is beginning to give birth to his inner self. Paradoxically, I am heartened by his not being completely changed at the end, because I wouldn't trust that, given who he is at the beginning of his story. Gilgamesh remains human.

The Epic of Gilgamesh has much to teach men about our lives and what we need to do to change our lives. It teaches us that to change we are going to have to also learn about ourselves from the women we know and from women's writings in every section of the library and bookstore. Gilgamesh would have stayed a static, cruel, one-dimensional tyrant had it not been for the intercession of mortal women and intervention of immortal women in his life. Gilgamesh also learned from Enkidu, who is a kind of shaman, wild man, or mythic Green Man. These archetypal shamanic men are not ordinary men who pass on the male-dominated mythology. They embrace and hold within themselves the realm of the sacred feminine. Their wisdom comes partly from the forest, nature, and Mother Earth. In Robert Bly's terms, these are places "far from the centers of ambition."[21] Enkidu was created and schooled by the goddesses and sent by them to transform Gilgamesh's life.

To find balance in our lives, we are going to have to directly address the imbalances. We will need to make ourselves available to *any* writings, experiences, wisdom, or insights that can restore harmony in ourselves and to our actions in the world. It seems clear to me that growing up in our culture we learn enough of the mythology of maleness. What we don't learn about is the wisdom of the sacred feminine. This is the wisdom the goddesses set about to teach Gilgamesh. For me, the essence of this feminine wisdom in *Gilgamesh* is his encounter with the pain of losing his dear friend Enkidu. The book runs counter to the male ethos. Gilgamesh does not bury his suffering and grief; he fully inhabits it and begins a long, deep journey into the underworld where he hopes to resolve it. His grief is his sacred wound. It teaches him about his humanness. If Gilgamesh were immortal, as he wishes to be, he would not be able to fully experience such grief. Grief is about being finite, about dying. The wound of his grief begins to teach him empathy for the others he has wounded.

We all have such a wound, flaw, failure, or source of pain in our lives. Rather than hide it or discount it as the stoic male ethos would have us do, *The Epic of Gilgamesh* shows us the value of fully owning it and inhabiting it for what it can teach us. For me, this is the greatest value of this ancient work. Gilgamesh transforms his woundedness, his vulnerability, his weakness as a man into the beginnings of changed life as a human being. At the beginning of the story he is simply an icon of lifeless machismo. By the end, he has become a flesh-and-blood person. As I connect with his whole story, I feel part of a brotherhood that affirms change and hope.

[1] *The Epic of Gilgamesh, An English Version*, with an Introduction by N. K. Sandars (New York: Penguin, 1981), p. 62. Hereafter all numbers in parentheses are page numbers from this edition.

[2] Sylvia Brinton Perera, *Descent to the Goddess* (Toronto: Inner City Books, 1981), p. 84.

[3] *Gilgamesh*, edited and translated by John Gardner and John Maier (New York: Alfred A. Knopf, 1984), p. 71.

[4] Marija Gimbutas, *The Goddesses and Gods of Old Europe* (Berkeley, CA: University of California Press, 1982), p. 199 and *passim*.

[5] "Temple prostitution was a widespread phenomenon in the ancient world, and prostitutes and sexual inverts of various sorts are frequently associated with the Great Goddess." *Gilgamesh*, Gardner and Maier, p. 76, n. 19.

[6] Ninsun is a goddess noted for her wisdom and as a manifestation of the sacred feminine. It makes sense that she would explain to Gilgamesh the contents of his unconscious.

[7] *Gilgamesh*, Gardner and Maier, p. 86.

[8] Perera, p. 13.

[9] "The sheepfold, with its deep association of divinity and the sacred marriage, celebrated in poetry and ritual of Inanna (Ishtar) and Dumuzi (Tammuz), is the place of fertility and life, the natural place; but it is also the first step toward domestication." *Gilgamesh*, Gardner and Maier, p. 92.

[10] Erich Neumann, "On the Moon and Matriarchal Consciousness," *Dynamic Aspects of the Psyche* (New York: The Analytical Psychology Club, 1956), p. 57.

[11] *Matthew* 16:19; 18:18.

[12] C. G. Jung, *Aspects of the Feminine* (Princeton, NJ: Princeton University Press, 1982), p. 65.

[13] Perera, p. 89.

[14] Neumann, p. 49.

[15] Martin Buber, *I And Thou*, translated by Walter Kaufman (New York: Charles Scribner's Sons, 1970), p. 91.

[16] Ann and Barry Ulanov, *Religion and the Unconscious* (Philadelphia: The Westminster Press, 1975), p. 81.

[17] Joseph Campbell, *The Hero With a Thousand Faces* (Princeton, NJ: Princeton University Press, 1973), p. 185.

[18] Ann Belford Ulanov, *The Feminine in Jungian Psychology and Christian Theology* (Evanston, IL: Northwestern University Press, 1971), p. 304.

[19] Campbell, p. 187.

[20] Marija Gimbutas connects the snake as "the vehicle of immortality" (p. 95) with the Great Goddess in numerous places throughout *The Goddesses and Gods of Old Europe*.

2

Death of a Salesman

The truth, the first truth, probably, is that we are all connected, watching one another. Even the trees.

—*Arthur Miller*

Why should we honor those that die upon the field of battle, a man may show as reckless a courage in entering into the abyss of himself.

—*W. B. Yeats*

This Pulitzer Prize-winning play (1949) introduces salesman Willy Loman. Willy has traveled over a million miles in his lifetime covering his routes in New England, but he has never taken a single step into his interior life. He lives his life seeking success and approval in the eyes of others. In the two acts and the requiem of the play, we see Willy attempting to transfer his values to his favorite son, Biff. Now in his thirties, Biff is deeply in conflict between wanting to please his father and recognizing that the life he has chosen makes him a man his father cannot take pride in. When Willy realizes that he is no longer a success-ful salesman, he kills himself in a final desperate act, hoping that the insurance money will somehow make Biff into someone important.

The landscape of *Death of a Salesman* is devoid of nature in both its immediate setting and the larger context of the play. Around Willy Loman's house, now surrounded by tall apartment buildings, "The grass don't grow any more, you can't raise a carrot in the back yard."[1] In that sterility there is a deep absence of the feminine. Nothing will grow, and the "two beautiful elm trees" (p. 17) that once graced Willy's yard have been cut down. There is no sense of the sacred in nature and no sense of nature's presence in the women or men in the play. Here in the mid-twentieth-century setting of the play, the ambitious, approval-seeking values of the patriarchy are no longer balanced by the more personal values of the feminine. The patriarchy has won out, and its monolithic life-denying values have enveloped the women and the men, reminding us of Sylvia Perera's observation that in our time women often become puppets of the patriarchy, victims of its devaluation and driving out of the feminine in all of us.

Death of a Salesman offers a stark, terrifying portrayal of a male-dominated culture and of people who accept its values and don't have a clue as to why they're lost and empty. Gilgamesh, to the extent that he begins to recover his humanity, does so because of the intercession of a host of women, mortal and divine, who represent the literal and figurative voices of the feminine. Gilgamesh encounters and is enlightened by women who are wise in the ways of the feminine. Aruru creates Gilgamesh's double in Enkidu, his mother Ninsun interprets his dreams, a temple prostitute educates Enkidu in "the woman's art," the winemaker Siduri encourages him to live his mortal life to the fullest, Utnapishtim's wife directs Gilgamesh to the sacred rose, and the goddess Ishtar intervenes on his behalf. In *The Epic of Gilgamesh* and its time, the feminine was still present as a viable balancing power in an increasingly male-dominated culture. As Samuel Kramer points out, "The goddesses of Sumer played a crucial, pivotal role in Sumerian religion to the very end—God in Sumer never became all male."[2]

Willy and his sons Biff and Happy have no access to this balancing force. There are no such women in *Death of a Salesman*. Linda, Willy's wife, feeds the needs of his pathetically inflated ego. Willy's ego is externalized, dedicated to superficial male bravado, making an impression, and seeking approval from other men. In his sixties he presents a sad, frayed mask of a self that cannot conceal the abyss of his inner emptiness. Linda has recognized his inner poverty all along but has generally helped Willy to perpetuate his self-fiction. She says to Biff, "And be sweet to him tonight, dear. Be loving to him. Because he's only a little boat looking for a harbor"[3] (p. 76). Miller introduces her in his stage directions as "Most often jovial, she has developed an iron repression of her exceptions to Willy's behavior . . . ." (p. 12). In becoming the dutiful wife, Linda has swallowed a dose of patriarchal poison as well. She has repressed her feelings and her inward knowledge of Willy so deeply that standing at his graveside in the Requiem, she is at first unable to cry: "Forgive me, dear. I can't cry. I don't know what it is, but I can't cry. I don't understand it. It seems to me that you're just on another trip. I keep expecting you. Willy, dear, I can't cry" (p. 139).

Willy Loman's lack of an authentic self is on a grand scale; it is truly *epic*. No one in literature seems as hollow as Willy Loman. His work, his values, his family, and his culture are profoundly hollow. What makes the play so terrifying is that all of this is so *ordinary*, a typically all-American model of life.

Willy is a salesman, a "road man" (p. 80) who, since the age of eighteen, has logged perhaps a million miles covering his routes in New England. When the play opens, he is lost, barely able to drive his car on the highway safely. He has lost his customers, and he doesn't know what "the secret" (p. 92) is anymore. Willy is an ordinary man who has played by the rules and doesn't know why he is lost, a failure. Over and over again in the play he asks other men: "What—what's the secret?" (p. 92).

If *The Epic of Gilgamesh* is about Gilgamesh's failed quest for the secret of immortality, *Death of a Salesman* is about Willy Loman's failed quest for the secret of male success. Willy addresses his brother saying, "Ben! I've been waiting for you so long! What's the answer? How did you do it?" (p. 47). Gilgamesh, even though he ignores the advice, is repeatedly told *not* to seek immortality but to pursue the "secret" of *mortality*, of living in the present. Five thousand years later, Willy Loman still struggles with a patriarchal view of time. Willy lives for the future or in a misty, illusory past—never in the present. "Dad is never so happy as when he's looking forward to something!" (p. 105). Willy has no idea how to live in the reality of the present because he can't live in the reality of himself. Linda says to Biff, his favorite son, "When you write you're coming, he's all smiles and talks about the future, and he's just wonderful. And then the closer you seem to come, the more shaky he gets, and then, by the time you get here, he's arguing, and he seems angry at you. I think it's just that maybe he can't bring himself to—to open up to you" (p. 54).

Willy wants Biff to be the man Willy isn't, to win for Willy the public approbation he seeks and has never attained. Biff isn't a replacement for Willy, and Willy can't see Biff for the man he is. In fact, Biff has begun to make a *real* life for himself, "to find himself" (p. 16). Biff has been working out west on a farm in contact with the earth, crops, and animals—all aspects of the sacred feminine missing from Willy's life. Willy can't acknowledge the reality of Biff's life or show Biff love and approval in the present. As Biff says, "Dad, you're never going to see what I am, so what's the use of arguing?" (p. 129).

One of the terrible legacies of our culture, especially for men, is "trophy hunting." We seek the outward manifestations of success without regard for the inward corollaries and pay the price of inner emptiness. Like Willy, we believe "it's not what you do. . . . It's who you know and the smile on your face! It's contacts . . . contacts!" (p. 86). Willy seeks the contacts, appearances, good first impressions, "being well liked"; these are his trophies. What his life is like, how he feels about it, what he's like inside, and the quality of his relationships with himself and others are all invisible—not things, and therefore of no real value to him. In The *Epic of Gilgamesh* we learn that Gilgamesh makes a mistake seeking the illusory prize, the flower of immortality, at the expense and loss of the invisible, intangible prize of simply being alive.

The stage directions for *Death of a Salesman* include Miller's description of the set: "To the right of the kitchen, on a level raised two feet, is a bedroom furnished only with a brass bedstead and a straight chair. On a shelf over the bed, a silver athletic trophy stands" (p. 11). In such a deliberately sparse, empty set the trophy stands out as a totem for the whole play. Willy has always wanted Biff to build a life out of that trophy, to make the physical emblem of his athletic accomplishments symbolic of his whole being. To Willy, the moment when Biff earned the trophy made him "like a young god. Hercules—something like that. And the sun, the sun all around him. Remember how he waved to me? Right up from the field, with the representatives of three colleges standing by? And the buyers I brought, and the cheers when he came out—Loman, Loman, Loman! God Almighty, he'll be great yet" (p. 69).

Gilgamesh, who has no wife or family, only misses the experience of a better life for himself. Willy misses much more because he fails to connect with Biff, Happy, Linda, and his own life. Biff is struggling to find a real connection to himself, his life, and his work—to be authentic. Even though he has begun to find this in his life as a farmhand, his father's patriarchal value system intrudes and makes it difficult for Biff to cherish his life and what it means to him. After a failed visit to set up a business deal for which he is unsuited, Biff reflects, "Suddenly I stopped . . . I stopped in the middle of that building and I saw—the sky. I saw the things that I love in this world. The work and the food and the time to sit and smoke. . . . Why am I trying to become what I don't want to be? . . . when all I want is out there, waiting for me the minute I say I know who I am! Why can't I say that to Willy?" (p. 132). Biff can't say it because it all relates to nature, feelings, a feminine sense of time, and staying in the present. It flies in the face of all that he has learned from his father and his father's culture. Biff is like one of the seeds that can't grow in his father's world. He is full of life, full of potential, but has never been given a context in which to germinate and grow.

Biff is a modern representative of the archetype of the Green Man in that he longs to return to his regenerative work on a ranch out west; his rejection of his father's values when he defiantly asserts, "I'm not bringing home any prizes anymore, and you're going to stop waiting for me to bring them home!" (p. 32) is a major turning point in *Death of a Salesman*. When Biff speaks to his brother Happy about his life out west, the tension between his experiences with the feminine in nature and his patriarchal expectations of what he should want for himself are clearly underscored:

> This farm I work on, it's spring there now, see? And they've got
> about fifteen new colts. There's nothing more inspiring or—beautiful
> than the sight of a mare and a new colt. And it's cool there now, see?
> Texas is cool now, and it's spring. And . . . suddenly I get the feeling,
> my god, I'm not gettin' anywhere! What the hell am I doing, playing
> around with horses. . . . I oughta be makin' my future. That's when I
> come running home. And now, I get here, and I don't know what to
> do with myself. (p. 22)

Out west, Biff is happy making his present, not his future. It is rich, alive, and satisfying, but he has little or nothing to show for it. In his father's value system, "A man has got to add up to something" (p. 125). A daily life of personal, internal satisfaction doesn't add up to something Willy or Biff can put on a shelf like a trophy.

Presumably, after Willy's death, Biff will go back out west and live the potentially integrated life he loves in harmony with sky, earth, animals, and his own feminine side. Biff embraces what is absent in Willy's life. Near the end of the second act, Willy rushes off quite agitated "to get some seeds, "I've got to get some seeds, right away. Nothing's planted. I don't have a thing in the ground" (p. 122). A short time later we see Willy trying to plant a garden in the dark of night by flashlight, but for him it is too late. Willy can't get anything to grow because he has dedicated himself so much to externals that he has no interior life. Willy has nothing growing in the ground because there is nothing growing *in him*. This is one of the strongest, most important dimensions of the feminine—its dark, internal, subjective, procreative dimension. In the play, Miller represents the denial of the feminine principle of the womb, earth, and psyche as "seeds" whose internal and unconscious contents are unable to grow. Linda says of Willy, "a lot of people think he's lost his balance" (p. 56). Willy's utter devotion to the surfaces of things, to the secrets of success—"it's not what you say, it's how you say it" (p. 65); "it's not what you do . . . it's who you know" (p. 86)— reveals that he is completely unbalanced. He is a victim of the most shallow values of a patriarchal, materialist, careerist, male-dominated culture. He venerates "selling [as] the greatest career a man could want" (p. 81).

In a person so committed to blocking out and ignoring the internal self, the feminine nature can appear in consciousness only by force, by making its own "unscheduled" appearances. By implication, the insight is that if one makes no room in one's life for the feminine it will show up unannounced on the doorstep. Early on, Willy reports to Linda that when he drives he is often suddenly dangerously distracted from within: "All of a sudden I'm goin' off the road! I'm tellin' ya, I absolutely forgot I was driving. . . . So I went on again—and five minutes later I'm dreamin' again, and I nearly—*He presses his fingers against his eyes.* I have such thoughts, such strange thoughts" (p. 14).

Music, a strong signature of feminine consciousness, is given a subtle but continuous role throughout the play. There are some eighteen stage directions for it, beginning at the opening of Act One where music is strongly linked with nature, which is otherwise absent: "A melody is heard, played upon a flute.[4] It is small and fine, telling of grass and trees on the horizon. The curtain rises" (p. 14). Significantly, these same stage directions make a kind of character direction a bit further on: "From the right, Willy Loman, the Salesman, enters, carrying two large sample cases. The flute plays on. *He hears but is not aware of it*" (p. 12; italics mine). Willy's world is so devoid of the feminine that even when one of its voices is audible, he remains unaware of it. Learning to listen inwardly and outwardly is one of the powers conveyed by the divine feminine, and Willy is not a listener. For example, he ignores the female voice of the telephone operator repeatedly calling him in his hotel room in Boston. This inability to hear and respond to the feminine is crucial to an understanding of Willy's failures in his relationships with others. Throughout the play the feminine makes even stronger appearances in what are called Willy's "imaginings" (p. 12), those dramatized scenarios from the past that are like visions superimposed on the present.

The imaginings are revelations of his past that are seen by Willy and the audience, but not by Linda and the boys. Willy's brother Ben appears in one of these sequences; and we learn that when Willy started out as a salesman, Ben went into the jungle, discovered a diamond mine, and became rich. For Willy, this memory underscores the smallness of his own life. In another, we discover the root of Biff's inability to value his father's example. Biff fails math in his senior year of high school; and unless he can get his father to convince the teacher to change his grade, Biff will be ineligible for any of the athletic scholarships he has been offered. Biff makes an unannounced trip to Boston to seek his father's help and discovers Willy in his hotel room with a prostitute. The contrast between his father's duplicity and his stated values drives Biff forward on a lonely path to create an authentic life for himself. These tableaux from the past illuminate Willy's history and reveal his crowded and troubled present. Like the music that at times "insinuates itself" (p. 27) into the action, these dramatic enactments of Willy's inner life appear of their own accord, against his wishes.[5] In the end, these dark contents of his unconscious overwhelm and engulf him, leading to his suicide. Willy's final utterance in the play is not even a word, just the terrible, tragic cry of "Shhh!" made in desperation to quiet these inner voices. These are the voices of the feminine he has refused to listen to throughout his entire life, welling up into an interior cacophony:

Willy, *uttering a gasp of fear, whirling about as if to quiet [Linda]*:
"Sh!" He turns around as if to find his way; sounds, faces, voices,
seem to be swarming in upon him and he flicks at them, crying, "Sh!
Sh!" Suddenly, music, faint and high stops him. It rises in intensity,
almost to an unbearable scream. He goes up and down on his toes,
and rushes off around the house. "Shhh!" (p. 136)

In the opening stage direction for music "telling" of nature, and in Willy's
anguished final "Shhh!" to silence the voices of the sacred feminine
within him, lie the alpha and omega of his tragedy.

Personal Commentary

Today, everything and everybody is for sale. Very few of us can avoid
having to sell something or to market ourselves. When Willy Loman is
referred to in the play in archetypal terms as "the Salesman" (p. 12), it
is because he represents all of us. We never learn what he sells because
it doesn't matter. His profession, which is also his plight, touches us all.

I hoped to escape this circumstance by becoming a college teacher,
but today colleges and universities increasingly regard themselves as
businesses. Departments, courses, and subjects are frequently appraised
in marketing terms. Enrollment numbers, popularity, what sells, staying competitive—these are the business concerns that have found their
way into academia. My students often speak of having to "package"
and "market" themselves with the courses and extracurricular activities
they take on. They ask, "What will a prospective employer think of me
if I take a poetry writing class and join a 'Men Against Violence Against
Women' group? Wouldn't I look better to employers if I took another
economics course and joined the Business Club?" Shades of Willy
Loman.

The play was first produced in 1949 and it has a few minor anach-
ronisms—the Studebaker is no longer with us and microcassette re-
corders have replaced the dictaphone—but by and large the play is remarkably timely in its warning that each of us may become so caught
up in marketing our outer selves that we lose our very souls. Willy's
tragedy is that he plays by the rules of the patriarchy and its values,
ignoring and not understanding "the secret" it keeps from us—namely,
that just as we must work hard to be outwardly successful, we must
work equally hard to have inner lives that nurture, keep, and give birth

to our souls. We need to "have something in the ground." Women give birth to children, but men and women both must give birth to themselves, to have authentic inner selves. A great deal of the anger and pain that men feel in our culture stems from being denied access to that kind of birthing process within the values of a male-dominated culture.

Willy Loman is frightening because he has no soul and doesn't even know it. He has lost touch with his own soul-making inner resources and processes. He has no creative life; he doesn't work with his hands, he has no garden—he has nothing to do except be a salesman, a former salesman. He has not been about the business of soul-making, of giving birth to his inner life and maintaining it. To his way of thinking, why should he? There's no money in it, no success, no popularity, nothing marketable. This is why he can't value what Biff has found in his work as a farmhand out west. It is the very kind of work that may well save Biff from becoming like his father and may give Biff his soul—but because it doesn't amount to much financially, neither Willy nor Biff knows how to properly value and cherish it. Willy can't really even father his sons, he can't show them how to find their inner selves or show them that men have to be both strong and nurturing.

In Matthew Fox's terms we, like Willy Loman, have let the patriarchy dominate our psyches until it is killing off the feminine in us. Fox maintains that the reigning disease of our time is patriarchy, and "its symptom is matricide, the killing of the maternal in and all around us."[6] It is the disease that took down Willy's beloved elm trees, killed the garden in his yard and in himself, and finally kills him. *Death of a Salesman* is a powerful warning about the symptoms of a disease that has the potential to kill all of us.

[1] Arthur Miller, *Death of a Salesman* (New York: Viking Press, 1960), p. 17. Hereafter all numbers in parentheses are page numbers from this edition.

[2] Samuel Noah Kramer, *From the Poetry of Sumer* (Berkeley, CA: University of California Press, 1979), p. 71.

[3] This metaphor is striking in its applicability to the material in the next chapter—Odysseus' ten-year quest to get home to his own "safe harbor" of Penelope and Ithaca—this "safe harbor" being an obvious reflection of feminine space with its containment, acceptance, and protection.

[4] I don't want to make too much of this, but it seems worth noting that at least one source says of the flute that it embodies a form of wholeness: "The complexity of its symbolism derives from the fact that, if, by virtue of its shape, it seems to have a phallic significance, its tone is nevertheless related to inner, feminine intuitive feeling (that is, to the anima)." J. E. Cirlot, *A Dictionary of Symbols* (New York: Philosophical

Library, 1962), p. 105. In the play (p. 49), we learn that Willy's father *sold* flutes.

[5] Here attention should be drawn to the full title of the play, a detail which is sometimes overlooked: "Death of a Salesman: Certain private conversations in two acts and a requiem."

[6] Matthew Fox, *The Coming of the Cosmic Christ* (New York: Harper & Row, 1988), p. 81.

3

The Odyssey

Androgyny is an archaic and universal formula for the expression of *wholeness*, the coexistence of the contraries.

—*Mircea Eliade*

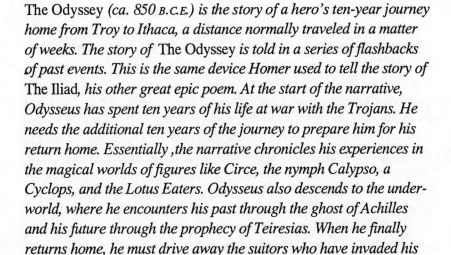

The Odyssey *(ca. 850 B.C.E.) is the story of a hero's ten-year journey home from Troy to Ithaca, a distance normally traveled in a matter of weeks. The story of* The Odyssey *is told in a series of flashbacks of past events. This is the same device Homer used to tell the story of* The Iliad, *his other great epic poem. At the start of the narrative, Odysseus has spent ten years of his life at war with the Trojans. He needs the additional ten years of the journey to prepare him for his return home. Essentially ,the narrative chronicles his experiences in the magical worlds of figures like Circe, the nymph Calypso, a Cyclops, and the Lotus Eaters. Odysseus also descends to the underworld, where he encounters his past through the ghost of Achilles and his future through the prophecy of Teiresias. When he finally returns home, he must drive away the suitors who have invaded his home and pursued his wife Penelope during his absence. Only then can he begin the actual process of creating a peaceful family life.*

Odysseus is a man receptive to paradox. He allows himself to experience the *hierosgamos* and through it becomes a more evolved man. *The Odyssey* is very much about Odysseus' efforts to reclaim himself, his home, his wife, his son, and his family life. *The Odyssey* can be seen as the story of one man's struggle to recover what Ann Belford Ulanov calls the "modality of being" which is the feminine.[1] It is this way of being that Odysseus has lost during the ten years of the Trojan War.

In her essay "The *Iliad* or The Poem of Force," Simone Weil asserts that "the true hero, the true subject, the center of the *Iliad* is force . . . force [that] turns anybody who is subjected to it into a thing . . . it turns a man into a stone."[2] This is true, she argues, of both those who employ force, those intoxicated by it, and those who are its victims. As Weil says, "Violence obliterates anybody who feels its touch."[3] Odysseus is no exception. Book Nine of *The Odyssey* relates how immediately after leaving Troy, a city and a people now destroyed, Odysseus and his men were brought *randomly,* by the wind, to Ismaros, where for no particular reason they "stormed that place and killed the men who fought. Plunder we took, and we enslaved the women . . . ." (p. 146).[4] After ten years at war with the Trojans, he is so corrupted by violence that he and his warriors sack a city without provocation, killing people who are not his enemies.

After ten years of functioning as a thing destroying other things, Odysseus' struggle to return home reflects his efforts to recover from the petrification of war. One clear sign that he is turning from a stone back into a feeling person is his sometimes open, sometimes concealed weeping. He weeps for his home and his wife Penelope during all seven years on Calypso's island. Odysseus recalls, "Immortal clothing I had from her, and kept it wet with tears" (p. 118). When he is with the Phaeacians, a minstrel sings of the Trojan War; Odysseus covers his face with his cloak to hide his weeping. Later the minstrel sings of the famous episode of the Trojan horse in which Odysseus and a band of Greek soldiers hid. When it was dragged inside the walls, the Greeks finally penetrated Troy, and the defeat of the Trojans soon followed. Hearing this, Odysseus weeps more openly. He can only be weeping for the death and destruction he was a party to:

> And Odysseus
> let the bright molten tears run down his cheeks,

> weeping the way a wife mourns for her lord
> on the lost field where he has gone down fighting
> the day of wrath that came upon his children.
> At sight of the man panting and dying there,
> she slips down to enfold him, crying out;
> then feels the spears, prodding her back and shoulders,
> and goes bound into slavery and grief.
> Piteous weeping wears away her cheeks;
> but no more piteous than Odysseus' tears. . . . (pp. 140–41)

The striking analogy made here between Odysseus' weeping and the weeping of a woman who has lost her husband in battle and is now to be carried off into slavery reveals how much Odysseus now feels for the victims of his days as a warrior. It reveals how much Odysseus' life since leaving Troy has been reshaped by the sacred feminine.

At the very end of the poem, when he has passed every test to prove to Penelope that he is who he says he is and she accepts him, first he cries openly and then, appropriately and symbolically, they weep *together:*

> Now from his breast into his eyes the ache
> of longing mounted, and he wept at last,
> his dear wife, clear and faithful, in his arms,
> longed for
>   as the sunwarmed earth is longed for by a swimmer
> spent in rough water where his ship went down
>   . . .
> and so she too rejoiced, her gaze upon her husband,
> her white arms round him pressed as though forever.
> The rose of Dawn might have found them weeping still
> had not grey-eyed Athena slowed the night. . . . (pp. 436-37)

It is important to read *The Odyssey* remembering *The Iliad,* or at least with a sense of the Trojan War that preceded it; for it is from that deadening "empire of force" that *The Odyssey* and its world of the sacred feminine retreats.

If we think of war as a single, logical, disastrous extension of the masculine principle, the principle of competition, aggression, self-aggrandizement, separation, and ultimate alienation from others, then *The*

Iliad chronicles it well. If we think of home as one embodiment of the feminine principle, representing relationship, community, cooperation, nonaggression, and the welfare of oneself and others, then *The Odyssey* chronicles the ten years it takes Odysseus to return "home" to Ithaca, to the feminine, from the masculine, destructive battle of Troy. The narrative presents his gradual inner turning from a masculine one-sidedness to a more balanced inner harmony with the sacred feminine. When he is nearly home, Odysseus says to the young woman Nausicaä, "the best thing in the world / being a strong house held in serenity / where man and wife agree" (p. 104). This strong house is both one's outer physical home and the androgynous psychic balance achieved when one is at home within oneself.

When we first meet Odysseus in Book Five, he is on the goddess Calypso's paradoxical island where he has spent the past seven years. In spite of Calypso's great beauty and her promise of immortality for Odysseus should he choose to remain with her, Odysseus still wants to return home. He is a man at peace with his mortal nature. He desires only to return to Ithaca and be reunited with his mortal wife Penelope. How different he is from Gilgamesh! Gilgamesh blatantly rejects the goddess Ishtar's offer of marriage. Odysseus is very sensitive in refusing Calypso's similar offer. When she is piqued at being rejected in favor of Penelope, Odysseus responds with great gentleness,

> My lady goddess, here is no cause for anger.
> My quiet Penelope—how well I know—
> would seem a shade before your majesty,
> death and old age being unknown to you,
> while she must die. Yet, it is true, each day
> I long for home, long for the sight of home. (p. 87)

The passage reveals both how well Odysseus knows himself and how much *The Odyssey* is a love story. If Odysseus didn't truly love Penelope and didn't know himself in and through that love, he could hardly pass up Calypso's offer of immortal life with her on her island paradise. The tension between his choices is dramatic and powerfully significant for the rest of the poem. He can choose paradise, eternal life, and marriage to the ageless, divine Calypso or continue his perilous return to Ithaca, where his home is presently besieged by suitors seeking to marry

Penelope. At Ithaca, ordinary mortal life, an aging Penelope, and his son Telemachus await him. Odysseus chooses all that messy humanity, conflict, and trouble. He returns home and restores order to his family, showing just how wise he has become in the ways of the feminine. Ann Ulanov writes:

> Feminine wisdom is bound to the earth, to organic and psychological growth, to living reality. It issues from one's instincts, from one's unconscious, from one's history and relationships. It is nonspeculative wisdom without illusions, and it is not idealistic in its approach to reality but prefers what actually is to what should or might be. Feminine wisdom nourishes, supports and develops the strongest possible ties to reality.[5]

Ironically, it is the seven years Odysseus spends with Calypso on Ogygia that educate him in the feminine wisdom that draws him home. A word about the complex chronology of *The Odyssey* is necessary to explain this. Many other readers of the poem have pointed out that the events recounted in *The Iliad* are linear and sequential in a way suited to its masculine spirit and world view. The history and events of Odysseus' journey home unfold circuitously, more like a series of spirals or encirclements, in a manner analogous to a feminine way of understanding.[6]

When we meet Odysseus in Book Five, his ten-year journey home from Troy is nearly over. He is at the end of his seven years with Calypso. In Book Nine and following books, he tells the Phaeacians of his adventures during the three years between his departure from Troy and landing on Calypso's island. In those three years Odysseus and his men encounter the Lotus Eaters, the Cyclops, the god of the winds Aeolus, the giant Laestrygonian cannibals, the goddess Circe and her enchantments, the wraiths of Hades, the Sirens, the perils of Scylla and Charybdis, and the sacred bulls of Helios. These adventures are presented as part of a large flashback narrated by Odysseus.

One of the things that most intrigues me about *The Odyssey* is the seven years Odysseus spends on Calypso's island after three years of experiencing one dramatic adventure after another. Why does Homer leave Odysseus on Ogygia for seven years before beginning the last leg of his journey home? Seven is a magical number in ancient numerology. It is "the number of the scholar, the philosopher, the mystic and the occultist. Sevens are natural recluses. They like to withdraw from the maddening bustle of the world and be alone to meditate and reflect."[7] Odysseus was a man of action, "that man skilled in all ways of contending" (p. 1). He is hardly a natural recluse, but Homer has him spend seven years on Ogygia. Why? It gives him time to reflect on the ten years spent at Troy, and the three tumultuous years filled with legendary adventures. It takes seven years for Odysseus to understand what has happened to him, to organically reflect and inwardly ripen. During these seven years Odysseus does not contend with anyone, does not make war, and does not struggle against any adversities. The seven years allow Odysseus to encounter the virtues of the feminine. He develops the qualities of patience and contemplation and healing and transforming insight. Moreover, those seven years are spent on an island that is described in some of the richest, most magical, and symbolic language used for any geography in the poem, language that is wonderfully suggestive of the feminine. Even Hermes, the god sent to Ogygia to bring about Odysseus' release, is moved by its beauty:

> [Hermes] stepped up to the cave. Divine Kalypso
> the mistress of the isle, was now at home.
> Upon her hearthstone a great fire blazing
> scented the farthest shores with cedar smoke
> and smoke of thyme, and singing high and low
> in her sweet voice, before her loom a-weaving,
> she passed her golden shuttle to and fro.
> A deep wood grew outside, with summer leaves
> of alder and black poplar, pungent cypress.
> Ornate birds here rested their stretched wings—
> horned owls, falcons, cormorants—long-tongued
> beachcombing birds, and followers of the sea.
> Around the smoothwalled cave a crooking vine
> held purple clusters under ply of green;
> and four springs, bubbling up near one another
> shallow and clear, took channels here and there
> through beds of violets and tender parsley.
> Even a god who found this place would gaze, and feel his heart beat
> with delight:
> so Hermes did; but when he had gazed his fill
> he entered the wide cave. . . .

> But he saw nothing of the great Odysseus,
> who sat apart, as a thousand times before,
> and racked his own heart groaning, with eyes wet
> scanning the bare horizon of the sea. (p. 83)

I have quoted this passage at length because it is so lush and dense in its depiction of a *sacred* space, a place not only given over to the divine feminine but given over to the archetype of the Great Goddess. Odysseus has landed on no run-of-the-mill island! At her loom, with her fire making far-reaching smoke like the axis mundi, in a great cave by the deep woods, surrounded by the plants and animals, and most striking of all, with those four springs bubbling up from deep inside the earth, Calypso is in every way an embodiment of the Great Goddess. She is a divine mediatrix between heaven, earth, and the underworld. The weaving, the trees, the owls, and the sea birds are all seen by scholars like Erich Neumann and Marija Gimbutas as emblems of the Great Goddess as a mythologem of the archetypal feminine.[8] Speaking not of the four springs but of the symbolic pattern of four, Gimbutas writes: ". . . fourfold compositions, archetypal of perpetual renewal or wholeness . . . are associated with the Great Goddess of Life and Death, and the Goddess of Vegetation. . . . Symbols of becoming . . . accompany four-fold designs. They do not depict the end result of wholeness but rather the continuous striving towards it, the active process of creation."[9]

What better place is there for Odysseus to spend seven years learning something about the wisdom of the feminine and its consciousness of patience, ripening, depth, and contemplation? After ten years in the barren, strife-torn, and blood-drenched wasteland of the plains of Troy, Odysseus *needs* these seven years at the home of the divine feminine, a place that stops even Hermes in his tracks while he gazes and takes it all in.

So it is my contention that for seven years Odysseus has been doing nothing. He has been practicing *wu wei,* a Taoist expression for an aspect of the feminine coined thousands of years before it was called the feminine; it was called the Tao, or the Way, "the hidden 'Mother' of all life and truth."[10] Ann Ulanov says that one of the ways of the feminine "is a way of submitting to a process, which is seen as simply happening and is not to be forced or achieved by an effort of the will. [This] quality of feminine activity is a mixture of attentiveness and contemplation."[11] This is close to the ancient Taoist notion of *wu wei*. Thomas Merton describes it as "not . . . inactivity but *perfect action*—because it is act without activity. In other words, it is action not carried out independently of Heaven and earth and in conflict with the dynamism of the whole, but in perfect harmony with the whole. . . . The other way, the way of conscious striving . . . is fundamentally a way of self-aggrandizement, and it is consequently bound to come into conflict with Tao."[12] This is what Odysseus does during his seven years on Ogygia. He learns by practicing the "nonaction" of openness, of attentiveness, of letting go, the action of perfect timing. When the family cat looks up from the kitchen floor at a piece of fish left on a counter, it is practicing *wu wei*. When it executes a perfect, graceful jump onto the counter that looks effortless and magical, it is *wu wei*, too. Timing is everything. Odysseus needs seven years in Calypso's sacred home to be ready to enter his own sacred home.

On Ogygia, Odysseus had much to think about before completing his journey home because so much had happened to him since he had gone away. Of the many adventures Odysseus had in the three years after leaving Troy and before coming to Calypso's island, the descent into Hades is the only one I want to examine here, and I will look at only two of his encounters there. His experience recalls the descent of Gilgamesh[13] and furthers Sylvia Perera's theory that descents into the subterranean depths of the feminine are appropriate and necessary for anyone denied this source of insight.

Odysseus' encounters with Teiresias and Achilles in Hades are of special interest because they seem to be profoundly inclusive for Odysseus. Achilles takes him back in time to the ten years of the war with the Trojans. Teiresias takes him forward in time to a point after he is safely home and has entered the last years of his life. These encounters are like two lenses through which Odysseus can look at his recent past and his future. Moreover, it is in Teiresias' prophecy and Achilles' poignant wish that we encounter the archetype of the Green Man and its earth wisdom. Both encounters carry such weight that Odysseus might well have spent his years on Ogygia reflecting on them alone, but he had the other meetings of people from his past in Hades as well as his adventures to ponder.

Odysseus travels to Hades on the advice of the goddess Circe, who determined through her magic that Odysseus must seek and obey the advice of the spirit of Teiresias to return home safely. Circe had enchanted some of Odysseus' men and turned them into pigs.[14] Protected by a magic herb given to him by Hermes, Odysseus is able to resist Circe's magic and compels her to restore his men to their human form. Odysseus becomes her lover, and he and his men stay with her for a year. She is a dangerous witch who is amazed that Odysseus can resist her enchantments; through her skill in magic and the occult arts, she directs him to travel to Hades.[15]

Once there, what makes Odysseus' encounter with Achilles so momentous is that the shade of Achilles speaks only a few words to Odysseus. Yet those words call everything about the Trojan War into question, including the heroics and Achilles' own honor. Now that Achilles is located in the chthonic realm of Hades and Persephone, he indicates that if he could live his life over, he would not serve only the male heroic ethos but live in harmony with the sacred feminine.

When Odysseus meets Achilles in Hades he is struck by how depressed and downcast he seems and he attempts to cheer him up with words about his fame, his reputation among the living, and consequently his power among the dead:

> But was there ever a man more blest by fortune
> than you, Akhilleus? Can there ever be?
> We ranked you with immortals in your lifetime,
> We Argives did, and here your power is royal
> among the dead men's shades. Think, then, Akhilleus:
> you need not be so pained by death. (p. 201)

To this Achilles responds with profound cynicism about his power and honor as a dead man:

> Let me hear no smooth talk
> of death from you, Odysseus, light of councils.
> Better, I say, to break sod as a farm hand
> for some poor country man, on iron rations,
> than lord it over all the exhausted dead. (p. 201)

In short, the great hero of *The Iliad* would rather be an anonymous farmhand—a nothing among men, but alive—than famous and dead. Achilles has acquired earth-centered wisdom too late to be of use for himself, but it is not too late to be of use to Odysseus. Speaking of this kind of knowledge of the feminine, Erich Neumann writes: ". . . feminine wisdom accords with no abstract, unrelated code of law by which dead stars or atoms circulate in empty space; it is a wisdom that is bound and stays bound to the earth, to organic growth. . . . Hence, matriarchal consciousness is the wisdom of the earth, of peasants and, naturally, of women."[16] This wisdom has been repressed, denigrated, and exiled from our consciousness, just as women themselves have for so long been exiles from the social hierarchy. Odysseus must descend to Hades, to that place called by Homer the home "of Death and pale Persephone" (p. 180) in order to learn of such wisdom. In his encounter with Teiresias, that legendary, blind, androgynous seer who is a man but spent seven years as a woman, Odysseus learns even more about its relationship to his own life.

Teiresias foretells Odysseus' whole future, his return home, and his vanquishing of the suitors; he then gives Odysseus a most visionary directive. He explains that after Odysseus' house is put in order, he must travel on foot over land carrying an oar. He must walk until he comes to where men live who do not know the sea and find the place where "some passerby will ask, "What winnowing fan is that upon your shoulder?" There he must "halt and implant [his] smooth oar in the turf" (p. 189); soon thereafter Odysseus will die an easeful death. At the spot where someone can confuse Odysseus' oar, "the instrument of his sea wanderings," "the symbol of his warrior life" with a farming tool, Odysseus is to plant it like a tree in the earth. Clearly, at that point, Odysseus' recovery from Troy and its warrior values will be complete, and his warrior's tool will become a tool of the harvest. The oar will become a tree that represents the *axis mundi;* the symbolic joining of heaven and earth.

His seven years on Ogygia not only give Odysseus time to reflect on his past and his future, it gives him the experience of another mode of time. Up to this point he has primarily known linear, quantifiable time. Kathryn Rabuzzi says this kind of time is "associated with masculine questing."[17] After Ogygia Odysseus presumably knows something about *waiting,* "a time experience radically at odds with the more accepted time patterns of Western culture."[18] This is the experience of time his wife Penelope has endured for the twenty years of his absence. Another function of this seven-year period is to let Odysseus experience some of what Penelope knows before they are reunited; while there are some definite values to this waiting mode, protracted, enforced waiting is repressive or, as Rabuzzi says, "demonic."[19] When Odysseus does finally enter his house to drive out the suitors who have turned Penelope's waiting into a kind of prison, his anger is fueled by his direct knowledge of what this kind of enforced constraint is like. It is time for them both to control their relationship with time itself. In ridding his house of the men laying siege to his wife (ironically, just as he and his men were in siege of Troy), he gives time back to Penelope and himself, to use and experience in whatever way they choose. If we think of Penelope as one of many figures representing the goddess in Homer, then by "liberating" her, Odysseus is also "liberating" the feminine in himself. The act of killing the suitors is then not just a heroic action in a series of heroic actions, it is a deeply symbolic act of self-liberation and affirmation of the new self Odysseus has realized in his ten-year return to the Goddess.

There are three things to note about Penelope's function as a repre-sentative of the Goddess. There is her weaving, the challenge of shoot-ing the arrow through twelve axe heads, and the secret of the marriage bed only Odysseus and Penelope know. Erich Neumann says of weaving, "The primordial mystery of weaving and spinning has also been expe-rienced in projection upon the Great Mother who weaves the web of life and spins the threads of fate, regardless whether she appears as one Great Spinstress or, as so frequently, in a lunar triad. . . . Thus the Great Goddesses are weavers." Circe and Calypso have looms, and Penelope also has one. She uses it to keep the suitors at bay by promising she'll consider marrying one of them (they all assume Odysseus is long dead) when she's finished with making the shroud she's weaving for Odysseus' father Laertes. She weaves by day, then at night she unravels the day's work, keeping her at her task for what seems like forever. Until she is found out, her cunning—which is the match of her husband's—works to control time, which controls her fate in regard to the suitors.

When her trickery is discovered, she is finally forced to decide among the one hundred and eight men who seek to marry her. She brings out Odysseus' great bow and has twelve axe heads lined up, "at intervals like a ship's ribbing. . . . The one who easily handles and strings the bow and shoots through all twelve axes I shall marry" (p. 371). It is not clear whether the axes in question are double-headed axes or not, but it is known that the *labyris,* or double-headed axe, is associated with the Great Goddess. Both Erich Neumann and Marija Gimbutas refer to this characteristic goddess symbol.[20] It seems like a small point anyway, because the whole task is impossible for everyone but Odysseus. None of the suitors can even string the bow, much less shoot an arrow through all twelve heads! This is clearly a task to be completed only by one who is suited to marry a goddess, and only Odysseus qualifies.

Finally, there is the marriage bed, which Odysseus made from a living olive tree. The tree is a strong symbol of the Great Goddess. Neumann writes, "The Great Earth Mother who brings forth all life from herself is eminently the mother of all vegetation. The fertility rituals and myths of the whole world are based upon this archetypal context. The center of this vegetative symbolism is the tree."[21] At the center of *The Odyssey*, Penelope guards and protects this tree, this symbol of her divinity and the divinity of their sacred marriage. Even after Odysseus has strung his bow, shot the arrow through the twelve axe heads (an enactment of the sun's course through the twelve houses of the zodiac), and killed all of the suitors, Penelope is still cautious about taking Odysseus to her bed. She tells him the bed has been moved, to which he responds angrily that since the bed is built into a tree, it could never be moved. Only the real Odysseus would have known this secret; Penelope is convinced, and they are at last united again. Odysseus' description of the bed he built deserves quoting:

> An old trunk of olive
> grew like a pillar on the building plot,
> and I laid out our bedroom round that tree,
> lined up the stone walls, built the walls and roof,
> gave it a doorway and smooth-fitting doors.
> . . . I planed [the bedposts],
> inlaid them all with silver, gold and ivory,
> and stretched a bed between—a pliant web
> of oxhide thongs dyed crimson.
>   There's our sign!
> . . . Their secret!
> (p. 435)

It is a beautiful bed—with its silver, gold, and ivory inlays, its web, its pillar reaching up toward heaven, its roots down into the earth. This is a bed befitting a *hierosgamos,* a sacred union of opposites, and it is a sign, a secret worthy of Odysseus' long struggles, his long education in the feminine which brought him here. But the bed is a *symbol* of the *hierosgamos,* it is not the sacred union itself. A great bed does not a great marriage make. This mythic bed is their sign and their secret, but it is *not* their relationship, their daily reality together.

No one changes by just having experiences. If we change at all, it is by reflecting on our experiences, giving them time to sink in. This is what the seven years with Calypso gave Odysseus; even so, at the conclusion of *The Odyssey* Odysseus is not yet whole, has not yet achieved androgynous inner balance. The momentum of the violence in the slaying of the suitors and those who assisted them drives Odysseus into planning with Telemachus to destroy the families of the suitors. If Athena hadn't stepped in to call a halt to this escalation, Odysseus would have continued in the mode of the warrior he knew so well, perhaps too well. It should be pointed out that Athena makes over *fifty* substantial interventions on behalf of Odysseus, stepping in at crucial moments in almost every major episode of the voyage. In a very real sense, *The Odyssey* is not the story of Odysseus; it is the story of Odysseus *and* Athena. Here is just one example:

> And now at last Odysseus would have perished,
> battered inhumanly, but he had the gift
> of self-possession from grey-eyed Athena. (p. 93)

For all that Odysseus has learned about finding a balance of psychic forces within himself, that balance is not a static condition. The wisdom of the feminine exists invisibly only in who we are internally and in how we act and relate to others. Men like Odysseus, who have been in service of the patriarchal ethos most of their lives, do not balance that ethos with intuitive wisdom easily or quickly. Odysseus is not a new man; he is a middle-aged king and semiretired general who, after a long journey and an education in feminine wisdom, now faces the more difficult and complex challenge of incorporating this wisdom into the realities of his life and his relationships at home. Compared with Ithaca, Ogygia was a place of retreat, a kind of ivory tower. It is one thing to learn about the feminine in paradise from a goddess with whom you have no messy commitments. It is quite another to bring this learning into practice in the hurly-burly of your daily homelife. It might even be that Odysseus plots to kill the suitors' families as a kind of escape from being home, a way of avoiding the realities of everyday life with Penelope, Telemachus, and his father Laertes.

Personal Commentary

As I indicated in my preface, Mark Van Doren was the most inspiring teacher I've known in the classroom. He loved reading and taught his students how to love reading as well. He did a most remarkable and educationally revolutionary thing: he allowed us, encouraged us, showed us how to feel when we read. When we read the books he assigned, he sternly ordered us not to distort, inflate, or falsify our true responses to them, whatever they were. Van Doren knew that by the time we were in college we had all learned well how to mask our feelings as we adopted as our own the views of others, namely the views of our teachers or the critics we read. Van Doren allowed us to *own* our views, our readings of books, and thereby to begin to *own* ourselves and those books. He took the view that if we were ever to become lifelong readers (which he felt should be a major goal of any education) we would need to become lovers of books. Lovers of anything must first be allowed to *feel* what they feel, to exercise and strengthen and nourish their genuine emotions. How simple and remarkably rare was this wisdom! And as young men of the late 1950s, how much we needed this wisdom.

In 1959 Mark Van Doren was about to retire from Columbia after a very distinguished career as a teacher—a teacher who outside the university was also a Pulitzer Prize-winning poet, novelist, book reviewer, film critic, and widely esteemed man of letters. Van Doren loved Odysseus and spoke of him in class as if he were very much alive today and as if he were a friend, someone Van Doren knew personally. Here was one of Columbia's most distinguished professors, a man in his mid-sixties you couldn't snicker or roll your eyes about, carrying on in class about his personal, emotional relationship with Odysseus! It was as spooky as it was stunning. Van Doren became for us a kind of shaman or magician, bringing the spirit of Odysseus alive in himself and thereby showing us how to do the same. He did this with every book we read. He said about Don Quixote, "I love him as much as any man I ever knew, but I know he was a nuisance. The Don was a great nuisance."

As students we learned to imitate Van Doren only in that we began to find our own ways of making authentic, personal, emotionally felt connections with what we read. He didn't care what we felt or what we wrote about in our papers as long as we were honest and connected our responses to the texts. He wanted to know where and how the book in question provided whatever it provoked in us.

At the time I personally didn't care much one way or another about Odysseus. And this worried me. I was in my late teens and made no connection at all with Odysseus' problems as a warrior, a king, a father, and a husband. Frankly, the only moment in the whole book that genuinely moved me was the small recognition scene near the story's end involving Odysseus and his dog, Argos. Argos has been on guard, so to speak, waiting for his master to come home the whole twenty years Odysseus has been gone. In order to get into his house undetected by the men who have moved into it in his absence, Odysseus must come in disguise and he must not acknowledge Argos, who could give away the disguise. So Odysseus ignores his dog and the dog dies—either of a broken heart, or released by the knowledge that his master is home, or both. We had such a beloved dog in our family and I was moved by this tiny scene and so, taking Van Doren at his word, I wrote about it. The essay would probably have been thought of by other faculty at the time as silly, hokey, too personal, too minor, or too unsophisticated. But Van Doren liked it and the other essays I wrote that term. Here for me was a new way of reading and writing about books. Because I was allowed to enter any book we read on my terms and find myself in it, it became *my* book. A small seed from each work was planted in me, and I didn't have to pretend to be interested in the major themes, the major critical issues, the major *anything*. Ironically, writing for that class was hard, harder than cranking out essays on major questions that were not my own. After years of learning to adopt the views of others, it can be quite difficult to discover your own.

Now, as a grown man closer to Van Doren's age at that time, I see that *The Odyssey* is still mine and the seed has grown so that I find much more of myself in it. This comes from the long view Van Doren took of education and of reading. What interests me now is finding that same long view in *The Odyssey* itself. Given his upbringing as a warrior, king, and patriarch, it will take Odysseus the rest of his life to find the balancing power of the feminine in himself. Great as he is in many respects, he has not "arrived," he is not finished, even though he is middle-aged himself. It will take him yet more time and trials before his oar, the symbol of his warrior self, is seen to be a winnowing fan or implement of agriculture. True to this long, slow, and organic view of the change toward balance, at the end of the poem we don't see Odysseus as a changed man so much as a changing man. He is still a warrior, but one now completely able to hear "the great voice of the goddess" (p. 461). Upon hearing that voice, he is moved and instructed by it. As Homer writes in the last stanza of the poem, "he yielded to her and his heart was glad" (p. 462).

If we are ever to become lifelong readers of books, we must begin honestly as amateurs, i.e., as lovers, readers with feeling. If we are to make a lifelong connection with the sacred feminine, we must hear her "great voice" and feel her in our hearts. It is the assumption of this book that the great voice of the Goddess can be heard in much of our literature if we can read it with feeling. As Van Doren once said, "The purpose of the liberal arts is to develop the power to read a book and to listen. These are very great powers."

[1] Ann Belford Ulanov, *The Feminine* (Evanston, IL: Northwestern University Press, 1971), p. 191.

[2] Simone Weil, "The *Iliad*, or The Poem of Force" (Wallingford, PA: Pendle Hill, 1981), pp. 3, 4.

[3] Ibid., p. 19.

[4] Homer, *The Odyssey*, translated by Robert Fitzgerald (New York: Anchor Books, 1963), p. 146. This is the text cited throughout, and page numbers appear in parentheses.

[5] Ulanov, p. 191.

[6] *Ibid.*, p. 170.

[7] Richard Cavendish, *The Black Arts* (New York: Capricorn Books, 1968), p. 52.

[8] Erich Neumann, *The Great Mother* (Princeton, NJ: Princeton University Press, 1974), pp. 48, 226 (weaving; trees); Marija Gimbutas, *The Goddesses and Gods of Old Europe* (Berkeley, CA: University of California Press, 1982), p. 144 (birds).

[9] Gimbutas, p. 91.

[10] Thomas Merton, *The Way of Chuang Tzu* (New York: New Directions, 1969), p. 26.

[11] Ulanov, pp. 172–73.

[12] Merton, p. 28; 24.

[13] In *Homer: A Collection of Critical Essays*, ed. by George Steiner and Robert Fagles (Englewood Cliffs, NJ: Prentice Hall, 1962), Steiner suggests (p. 10) that it is "probable" that Homer knew the *Gilgamesh* epic.

[14] Sylvia Perera, *The Descent to the Goddess* (Toronto: Inner City Books, 1981),

p. 7: "But it is towards her—and especially towards her culturally repressed aspects, those chthonic and chaotic, ineluctable depths—that the new individuating, yin-yang balanced ego must return to find its matrix and the embodied and flexible strength to be active and vulnerable, to stand its own ground and still to be empathetically related to others."

[15] Pigs are an ancient symbol of the Goddess because of their fertility. See Gimbutas, pp. 211–14.

[16] Joseph Campbell points out that Circe offers to guide Odysseus to the Underworld and that she functions as "his mystagogue" in her giving him various instructions. *Occidental Mythology*, New York: Viking, 1964, pps. 171, 172.

[17] Erich Neumann, "On the Moon and Matriarchal Consciousness," *Dynamic Aspects of the Psyche* (New York: The Analytical Psychology Club, 1956), pp. 56–57. Italics mine.

[18] Wendell Berry, *The Unsettling of America: Culture and Agriculture* (San Francisco, CA: Sierra Club, 1978), p. 129. Berry makes another excellent observation that when Odysseus finds his father, Laertes, he is "spading the earth around a young fruit tree" (p. 452), and that although he is a king, Laertes "has survived his son's absence . . . *as a peasant.* . . . In a time of disorder he has returned to the care of the earth, the foundation of life and hope" (pp. 128–29).

[19] Kathryn Allen Rabuzzi, *The Sacred and the Feminine* (New York: Seabury Press, 1982), p. 145.

[20] *Ibid.*

[21] Neumann, *The Great Mother*, p. 226.

[22] Neumann, *The Great Mother*, p. 226.

[23] Neumann, pp. 117, 180, 306; Gimbutas, pp. 186–87.

[24] Neumann, p. 46.

[25] Titus Burkhardt, "The Return of Ulysses," *Parabola*, vol. III, November, 1978, p. 20.

4

The Adventures of Huckleberry Finn

Everyone is a moon, and has a dark side which he never shows to
anybody.

—*Mark Twain*

The narrator of The Adventures of Huckleberry Finn *(1885) is a
fourteen-year-old boy who has been physically abused by his
father and emotionally abused by his culture. Things get so bad
that he fakes his own death in order to make a clean sweep and
start his life over. He teams up with a runaway slave named Jim;
together these two outsiders go down the Mississippi to seek
their similar and different needs for freedom. Along the way,
they experience many adventures and trials together and sepa-
rately. Finally it dawns on Huck that he is aiding and abetting a
criminal, an act that could send him to jail. Huck's dilemma is
the crux of the book. Will he be bad in the eyes of the culture and
help Jim reach freedom, or will he be good and turn Jim over to
the authorities? Huck passes this test and makes a commitment
to be an exile from society forever.*

Huck Finn's story is really a view of the male-dominated culture told by an outsider. Huck is just a boy, somewhere between ages twelve and fourteen. He has been on his own so much that he is practically an orphan. He is living by choice on the outer edge of respectability and civilization. Unlike Odysseus, who is as much creator of the culture as he is its inheritor, Huck isn't yet a part of the male-dominated culture. The circumstances of his life have kept him an exile. He is a semi-educated, nearly parentless social outcast who prefers to live close to nature. This is what saves him from being permanently cast in the patri-archal mold the way his compatriot Tom Sawyer is. Huck's story is not about acquiring the wisdom of the feminine, but about how he tests, uses, and expands the intuitive knowledge he already possesses on his odyssey down the Mississippi. From start to finish, almost everything in *Huckleberry Finn* revolves around an inner dialectic between what Huck intuitively understands of the feminine as opposed to what the patriarchal culture and its representatives, such as Tom Sawyer, Miss Watson, and the widow Douglas, are trying to teach him. Both Odysseus and Huck must contend with balancing the feminine with the expecta-tions of patriarchy, but Huck has a decided advantage in that he comes to this balancing act with a better inner balance at the start. What he learns is to trust deeply, believe in, and build his life around what he knows intuitively and what he absorbs from Jim about the sacred feminine and its power.

Throughout *Huckleberry Finn*, a major focus is Huck's struggle between the proscriptive patriarchal culture and his own highly per-sonal, intuitive "education." Huck often goes into the woods to think something over; in the context of nature his thinking is clearest and uniquely his own. What finally ensues is a great internal battle between conventional morality on the one hand and Huck's heart on the other. Huck must decide once and for all whether to return Jim to slavery by telling his owner Miss Watson where he is or to help Jim continue his flight to freedom. In Huck's mind, the first choice will clear his con-science and see that he gets to heaven; the second will send him to hell.

In *The Adventures of Tom Sawyer*, where we first meet Huck, we learn just how much of what he is and does is informed by what Nor Hall calls the "lumen naturale," the light of nature, a primary source of matristic wisdom.[1] She writes that this light is necessary for "under-standing how the material world cohere[s]," how it shows "the connections between things."[2] In both *Tom Sawyer* and *Huck Finn,* this involves knowing how to read the signs of nature with naturalistic cures for warts, ways of relating to dead spirits, and a whole host of ideas about spirituality from pagan folklore beliefs. When we first meet Huck in *The Adventures of Tom Sawyer,* he is carrying a dead cat, which, as he explains, when taken to a graveyard at midnight and thrown into the wind carrying the sounds of devils, will cure warts. He gets this cure from "old Mother Hopkins," whom Tom has heard others call a witch. This prompts Huck to respond vehemently, "Say! Why, Tom, I *know* she is."[3]

Huck is closely connected to witchcraft in the sense that modern practitioners use the term. Starhawk defines witchcraft as a goddess-centered religion:

> Witchcraft is a religion, perhaps the oldest religion extant in the West. Its origins go back before Christianity, Judaism, Islam—before Buddhism and Hinduism, as well, and it is very different from all the so-called great religions. The Old Religion, as we call it, is closer in spirit to Native American traditions or to the shamanism of the Artic. It is not based on dogma or a set of beliefs, nor on scriptures or a sacred book revealed by a great man. Witchcraft takes its teachings from nature, and reads inspiration in the movements of the sun, moon, and stars, the flight of birds, the slow growth of trees, and the cycles of the seasons.[4]

This description parallels Huck's own deep, personal connection with nature. It gets deeper and richer when Huck meets up with Jim and learns even more about it.

As the book opens, Huck has gone back to live with the widow Douglas to learn how to be respectable so that he can be a member of Tom Sawyer's gang. Tom's gang is a microcosm of the larger social order. Tom is a model of patriarchy with its codes, rules, and authorities. He wants to do everything, including his adventures, by the book. Tom can't even play without following some literary authority's example. In contrast, Huck is creating his own book as he narrates the text of *Huckleberry Finn,* a book whose contents are very much at odds with the prevailing culture. The conflict Huck experiences with society, even his good friend Tom, is the basic issue of the book. Edward Whitmont's book, *The Return of the Goddess,* sees this kind of struggle as a struggle to recover the Goddess, for the "patriarchal principle [is] 'Thou shalt' or 'shalt not' [whereas] the Goddess says 'You may— perhaps. It is for you to find out.'"[5] Whitmont goes on to say that "in relation to the newly emerging Feminine . . . as inner directed aware- ness" there is a "dialectical tension between individual and collective values," a tension that produces "the search . . . for the Grail, for one's life meaning, one's selfness."[6] This is precisely what Huck is about, and it is why he must tell his own story. In order to do this, Huck must trust his own inner authority, which he contacts alone in nature.

There is no better example of the tension Huck experiences be- tween the patriarchal church of St. Petersburg and what he knows of the Old Ways than what transpires in Chapter One of his story. The widow Douglas tries to teach Huck something about the Bible, which Huck refers to as "her book."[7] Huck is told about "Moses and the Bulrushers," about Heaven, "the good place," and Hell, "the bad place" (p. 4). The great irony here is that while in the eyes of Miss Watson and the widow Douglas Huck is spiritually and religiously ignorant, he is, in fact, deeply spiritual and regards the whole world as a sacred text to be *read*. Up in his room after the tutoring session with the widow and Miss Watson, Huck demonstrates just how well he can read the spiritual text of the natural world:

> The stars was shining, and the leaves rustled in the woods ever so
> mournful; and I heard an owl away off, who-whooing about some-
> body that was dead, and a whippowill and a dog crying about
> somebody that was going to die; and the wind was trying to whisper
> something to me and I couldn't make out what it was, and so it made
> the cold shivers run over me. (p. 5)

Huck accidentally flips a spider from his shoulder into the candle flame, where it perishes before he can rescue it. He understands this as "an awful bad sign and would fetch me some bad luck" and he quickly tries to ward it off: "I got up and turned around in my tracks three times and crossed my breast every time . . . but I hadn't ever heard anybody say it was any way to keep off bad luck when you'd killed a spider" (p. 5). Soon Huck's alcoholic, abusive father shows up and brings Huck a kind of painful, life-threatening bad luck.

In Chapter One, the parameters are drawn between the world of the fictional town of St. Petersburg, where the story opens, and the world of the Territory, a somewhat mythic place identified with nature and home to exiled Native Americans, where Huck goes at the book's close. St. Petersburg is a site of the patriarchy and identified with the Bible, the idea of the next life, Saint Peter and Heaven, itself a mythic place quite a bit more abstract and incorporeal than "the Territory." Miss Watson describes Heaven to Huck: "she said all a body would have to do there was to go around all day long with a harp and sing, forever and ever" (p. 4). St. Petersburg is a place of law and order, a place where even Tom Sawyer's gang is ruled by the laws and rules of books. Tom, like Miss Watson and the widow, lives his life by the book: "Why blame it all, we've got to do it. Don't I tell you it's in the books? Do you want to go to doing different from what's in the books, and get things all muddled up?" (p. 9). St. Petersburg is dedicated to the mythos of civilization. The Territory is dedicated to the mythos of a newly emerging culture. This largely open wilderness was Indian Territory in what is now western Oklahoma. It was in Twain's day still somewhat unexplored. In the novel it can be seen as a metaphor for the geography of the unconscious realm of the feminine. Huck's trip down the river is about his preparation for a new life there among the Cherokee and Seminoles, tribes dispossessed of their homes and driven into exile. Huck is also an exile, and his growing identification with nature and its spirituality may well make Indian Territory a fairly congenial place for him to live.

Life in St. Petersburg is difficult for Huck. He doesn't understand Miss Watson's religion, with its prayers for "spiritual gifts" (p. 11); he quickly tires of Tom Sawyer's games of "enchantments" which Huck dismisses when he says "all that stuff was only just one of Tom Sawyer's lies" (p. 14). The last straw is when Huck's alcoholic father takes him by force to a cabin where he whips him periodically. Huck really has no choice but to make his escape from Miss Watson, from Tom, and from his Pap—St. Petersburg holds nothing for him. In preparation for the transformational journey he is about to take down the Mississippi River, that long, wide, mythical force of divine nature[8], Huck stages his own murder. Huck symbolically kills his St. Petersburg self. He leaves the cabin in such a way that his father thinks that robbers broke in, killed Huck, and dragged his body into the river. Once the scene is set, Huck, with a canoe and provisions, waits on Jackson's Island for the news of his death to have its impact on the community so that he can begin a new life with a new identity. On the island, he meets Jim, a runaway slave who is also fleeing from St. Petersburg.

Both Jim and Huck are fleeing from ownership, from being "owned" by the patriarchy. In the eyes of the system of slavery, Jim is not a person, he is the property of someone else. Huck, too, is owned by his father. His Pap is trying to claim the money Huck owns as his share of the treasure found in *Tom Sawyer*. As Huck's Pap puts it: "Here's the law a-standing ready to take a man's son away from him . . . the law backs that old Judge Thatcher up and helps him to keep me out o' my *property*" (p. 24; italics mine). Huck is caught between two patriarchs: Judge Thatcher, who is trying to get Huck away from his drunken father, and Pap, who is making his claim on his son. From Huck's point of view, he loses either way. If he obeys the Judge, he'll only end up having to be respectable like Tom Sawyer (whom Twain once speculated would have grown up to become a lawyer). If Huck goes with his father, he'll be imprisoned and abused. Huck escapes them both and finds Jim, a disenfranchised male who will become his "true" father. Jim will help Huck to become fully himself, to become more connected to nature and its intuitive wisdom.

In Chapter Four, before Huck and Jim are forced to run for their lives, Huck learns of Jim's prophetic powers and consults him about his father and the future. Daniel Hoffman points out that Jim plays an important "role as seer and shaman, interpreter of the dark secrets of nature which the white folks in the church deny, secrets which Tom Sawyer and all the other romanticists along the Mississippi cannot discover."[9] Hoffman says that "Tom will never share Huck's secret wisdom or his freedom;"[10] I would add that Jim and Huck's shared secret wisdom is the wisdom of the feminine, itself a secret in this culture. Moreover, Jim and Huck are examples of the Green Man archetype. As Huck's teacher, Jim helps Huck deepen his already extensive connections with nature and the feminine.

While Huck and Jim are on Jackson's Island, Jim interprets the weather signs and predicts the coming of a bad storm. They move their camp to higher ground and into a cave, a "womb-like cavern."[11] Here Jim, "like a 'magus,'" instructs Huck in the lore of weather, in the omens of luck, in the "talismans of death."[12] "Jim knowed all kinds of signs" (p. 40).

Learning to read signs is part of what feminine wisdom is about.

Recovering the lost language of intuition, feelings, and the signs of nature that are invisible to so many of us now creates a vocabulary for the life we lead inside as well. Jim teaches Huck about the signs of nature at first; his deepest teachings for Huck will have to do with learning to read the signs of the heart. These signs are dramatically at odds with Huck's culturally conditioned conscience. Feminine wisdom is not about learning social codes of behavior or abiding by the public, outer voices about who to be or what to think. Feminine wisdom is about learning to go beneath the surface of respectability and make contact with what is inside, with what is really felt deep in the heart. In *Tom Sawyer,* this tension between accepted ways of being and individualistic ways of being is clearly set between Tom and Huck. Huck doesn't like living with the widow Douglas because "The widder eats by a bell; she goes to bed by a bell; she gets up by a bell—everything's so awful reg'lar a body can't stand it." Tom's response is typical of his conformity, "Well, everybody does that way, Huck." Huck's rejoinder wonderfully summarizes his connection with feminine wisdom and his struggle to maintain an individualistic way of being, "Tom, it don't make no difference. *I ain't everybody,* and I can't stand it" (p. 280; italics mine).

Huck's journey down the river may be thought of as an enumeration of the ways in which Huck "ain't everybody." Ironically, as he learns more about his profound differences from the collective "everybody," he impersonates over half a dozen other people, including an unsuccessful impersonation of a young girl, Sarah Williams. The impersonations reflect Huck's openness, understanding, empathy for other people, and his ability to adapt and change. Ann Belford Ulanov notes that empathy and understanding of others is, in feminine consciousness, "the process by which a self becomes possible. . . . The making of a self is not possible until there is full recognition of otherness. And that self must include both male and female elements."[13]

This kind of personal, inner openness and flexibility associated with the feminine brings us to the central, symbolic importance of the Mississippi itself. In the novel, the river may be thought of as a great emblem for the sacred feminine. The power of its ever-changing movement and its depth are the antithesis of the static, unchanging, absolute. Like the archetypal Goddess, the river is both creator and destroyer. The river appears to Huck as "so still and grand." At the same time, its great force, shifting depths, hidden boulders, and sunken logs are potentially deadly. In *Life on the Mississippi*, Twain describes learning to read the river, not for its calm-seeming surfaces, but for the slightest signs of the potentially dangerous contents of its interior depths: "The face of the water, in time, became a wonderful book—a book that was a dead language to the uneducated passenger, but which told its mind to me without reserve, delivering its most cherished secrets as clearly as if it uttered them with a voice. And [it was the] most dead-earnest of reading matter."[14]

As Huck and Jim go down the Mississippi on their raft, Huck is being schooled by the river as an objective correlative for interiority. The river becomes a symbol for the inner life and the transformative power of the sacred feminine. Twain knew this transformative power well, for he tells us that he came to know how to read beneath "the glories and the charms which the moon and the sun and the twilight wrought upon the river's face."[15] His knowledge of the river is thus paradoxical. Twain knows it for its double nature, a gathering of opposites into a "both-and" paradoxical reality, as opposed to a patriarchal "either-or" view. Ann Ulanov writes, "The feminine style of transformation is to seek the spirit in the hidden meaning of concrete happenings, to go down deep into personal events and into the dark, unknown places of our own emotions, where we find abundance of life in an intensity of our inward responses."[16] In connection with this dimension of the feminine, it is important to note that Huck and Jim do their traveling on the river by moonlight. As runaways, of course, they don't want to be seen; but symbolically this is the time of the feminine, the matriarchal consciousness with its knowledge of the darker sides of nature and reality. Erich Neumann points out in his essay that "Growth needs stillness and invisibility, not loudness and light. It is no accident that the symbols of patriarchal consciousness are daylight and the sun. . . . It is not under the burning rays of the sun but in the cool reflected light of the moon, when the darkness of unconsciousness is at the full, that the creative process fulfills itself; the night, not the day, is the time of procreation. . . . The moist night time is the time of sleep, but also of healing and recovery."[17]

Some of the most lyrical and significant moments in the book take place when Huck and Jim are floating down the river at night. Floating in his canoe down to Jackson's Island, Huck observes, "The sky looks ever so deep when you lay down on your back in the moonshine; I never knowed it before. And how far a body can hear on the water such nights!" (p. 31). Huck can see deeply into the night sky and hear far on earth, including "every word" of people talking on a ferry landing.

This is part of the wonderful inclusiveness of the feminine: the depths and mysteries of nature are opened to us; we are included in them. Once Huck and Jim are together on their way down the river, they are quieted by the presence of the natural mysteries of the night sky and at times speculate about them: "It was kind of solemn, drifting down the big still river, laying on our backs looking up at the stars, and we didn't even feel like talking loud, and it wasn't often that we laughed, only a little kind of a low chuckle" (p. 55). "It's lovely to live on a raft. We had the sky, up there, all speckled with stars, and we used to lay on our backs and look up at them and discuss about whether they was made, or only just happened. . . . Jim said the moon could a *laid* them." (p. 101)

It seems appropriate that Jim has this ancient awareness of the moon as a generative, maternal force. Jim's roots are clearly more in African culture than in the white European culture of his owners in America. In *Woman's Mysteries, Ancient and Modern,* M. Esther Harding points out that the Great Mother Goddess worshipped in Africa "is a goddess of the moon and partakes of the characteristics of the moon."[18] Moreover, Harding notes that in ancient tradition, "the moon is the cause of all growth and increase. It is literally the *power* of growth."[19]

Jim intuitively knows the moon to be a maternal force; he functions not only as a surrogate father for Huck, but as a guide who helps Huck discover this natural feminine wisdom as well. Jim is one of the humblest figures in the book yet, paradoxically, he is also the most whole and the most fully realized as a man. Jim is a man with great depth and a great soul. Jim teaches Huck about nature and its signs; and he loves, comforts, and protects him at times. By openly expressing his feelings to Huck, Jim also teaches Huck how to feel. In one of the book's most moving examples, Jim tells Huck how he once struck his four-year-old daughter Elizabeth for refusing to obey him, only to realize moments later that she didn't respond to his command because she was deaf as a result of a bout with scarlet fever. In stark, profound contrast to Huck's father, who never felt a shred of remorse for his regular beatings of Huck, Jim openly bares the pain: "Oh, Huck, I bust out a-cryin' en grab her up in my arms, en say, 'Oh, de po' little thing! de Lord God Amighty fogive po' ole Jim, kaze he never gwyne to fogive hisself as long's he live!' Oh, she was plumb deef en dumb, Huck, plumb deef en dumb—en I'd ben a-treat'n her so!" (pp. 131–32).[20]

In revealing his emotionally most painful failing, Jim opens himself to Huck and reveals a deep humanity. Jim has a caring, loving, compassionate humanity shown by no other character in the book. One of the crucial lessons for Huck in this confession is how quickly, how spontaneously, Jim drops his authoritarian stance as a stern father to weep and hug his daughter like a tender, loving mother. It is a lesson for Huck's heart, one he certainly never got from his father or anyone else. Huck will put this lesson to use later on in Jim's behalf. The lessons of the heart are never abstract; they circle back and change the texture of one's life with others.

In the context of the novel, the pre-Civil War years in the Midwest and South, Jim is a nonperson, a "nigger," a piece of property worth eight hundred dollars to Miss Watson. The novel depicts a racist culture, and Huck is as much a racist as anyone. When Huck is lying to Aunt Sally about an accident on the river, he says, "We blowed out a cylinder-head." She asks, "Good gracious! Anybody hurt?" Huck answers, "No'm. Killed a nigger" (p. 185). Huck's paradoxical moral breakthrough is set against the backdrop of the institution of slavery. In helping Jim gain his freedom, Huck is committing a capital offense. According to the laws and beliefs of the patriarchy, Huck is committing both a crime and a sin at once. His patriarchal conscience *wants* to turn Jim in, but the wisdom and depth of his expanding consciousness won't let him. Huck is torn between rules, laws, and the way "everybody else" does things in Missouri and the love, compassion, and wisdom of his own heart.

The crucial scene in the book has Huck writing a letter to Miss Watson telling her where she can find her "runaway nigger Jim." Writing this, Huck "felt good and all washed clean of sin for the first time . . . in my whole life . . ." (p. 179). He is conforming to a racist patriarchal, social, and religious context. But Huck's heart intervenes: "And [I] got to thinking over our trip down the river; and I see Jim before me, all the time, in the day, and in the night-time, sometimes moonlight, sometimes storms, and we a floating along, talking, and singing, and laughing. But somehow I couldn't seem to strike no places to harden me against him, but only the other kind" (p. 179). These other kind of places are in his heart as he experiences his love for Jim and remembers all the ways Jim has shown love for him. Huck remembers Jim's *voice*, which in this moment creates the feminine sense of otherness, "the time . . . he . . . said I was the best friend old Jim ever had in the world, and the *only* one he's got now; and then I happened to look around and I see that paper" (p. 179). Hearing Jim's voice Huck encounters a strong force, stronger than his written efforts to clear his conscience, and he is transformed. Huck honors the voice that speaks to him from his heart.

Huck's decision may be one of the most paradoxically catastrophic choices made by any character in literature. As he decides *not* to turn Jim in and to help Jim reach ultimate freedom in the free states, Huck is certain he is committing a terrible act that will send him to hell: "All right, then, I'll *go* to hell," he says ominously (p. 180). In this act of exile Huck becomes like Jim. Now they are both fools and committed criminals. Both are at the bottom of the social hierarchy, completely set against the patriarchy. Both are each other's *only* friend. We read all of this as ironic, but Huck's heroism is not ironic to him. He is exiled by his decision, and in this light we can understand why "lonesome" is one of the most often used words in the novel.[21] In fact, four pages after his momentous decision, as Huck arrives at the Phelps' farm where he is going to try to free Jim, we encounter a very striking passage:

> I went around and clumb over the back stile by the ashhopper, and started for the kitchen. When I got a little ways, I heard the dim hum of a spinning-wheel wailing along up and sinking along down again; and then I knowed for certain I wished I was dead—for that *is* the lonesomest sound in the whole world.
>
> I went right along, not fixing up any particular plan, but just trusting to Providence to put the right words in my mouth when the time come; for I'd noticed that Providence always did put the right words in my mouth, if I left it alone (p. 184).

There are several things to note here. Huck wishes he were dead because something important in him has died. He is very much alone. His decision to free Jim and thereby reject his conscience has made him an exile. He has turned his back on his patriarchal culture in a profound way. What has died in Huck is his childhood. He is now fully a man, a balanced adult human being who is risking everything to save another human being. It's no accident that Huck hears the spinning wheel as "the lonesomest sound in the whole world." Weaving and spinning are directly connected to the Goddess who weaves life into being and unravels it into death. Huck trusts Providence and behaves in a feminine mode that does not "fix up any particular plan" but trusts to the moment, trusts that the right words will appear "when the time come."[22] By letting go of his conscience and his chances of going to "the good place," Huck has stepped over and become exiled, like the Feminine has been. He has entered the realm of "the bad place" (the Underworld) and accepted a way of life that is based more on trusting Providence in the moment than on making plans for the future. He has stepped over into exile by himself, and this is why one of the first things he encounters is a highly charged scene with the sound, and the voice, of the Goddess.

In deciding to be a criminal and go to Hell in order to free Jim, Huck sets himself apart from his social universe, including his boyhood compatriot Tom Sawyer. The final chapters of the novel recount Tom Sawyer's elaborate scheme to 'free' Jim in a fashion befitting a romantic adventure story. They only serve to point up how far beyond Tom Sawyer Huck has grown. In this section, Tom clearly regards Jim as an object, a kind of stage prop in his private fantasy manipulation. To make matters worse, Tom knows that all along Jim has already been freed by Miss Watson. To Tom Sawyer, Jim is still not a human being, whereas Huck and Jim are now spiritually united.[23] Huck becomes more himself in his decision to take a risk for Jim's sake. This is one of the principles of the feminine—individualism that is deeply embedded in the individualism of others. The emerging feminine principle is about entering deeply enough into ourselves to encounter our connection to others, because we are all connected. As Jean Shinoda Bolen defines it, "The sense that we are all one and that we are all related to this Earth is the emerging archetype today.... This sense of affiliation is the principle of the feminine...."[24]

As Huck symbolically "descends" into Hell to rescue Jim, he is irrevocably committed to the feminine consciousness that Jim, the river, the moon, and the Territory represent. Jim's protective role is epitomized by the next-to-last paragraph of the book, where he informs Huck that the body they discovered in a wreck on the river early on in their travels, which Jim kept Huck from seeing, was Huck's father. Jim is the last person in the novel to speak to Huck, and it is his loving voice that Huck will take with him into the Territory. Huck now knows much more of nature and himself because of Jim's teachings. Like a true Green Man, Huck is so closely identified with nature at the book's end that T. S. Eliot says, "He is in a state of nature. . . ."[25] In contrast, Tom Sawyer appears on the last page of the novel with a trophy, a bullet removed from his leg, which he wears "around his neck on a watch guard for a watch, and [he] is always seeing what time it is . . ." (p. 245). The trophy/bullet/watch fob is the perfect emblem for Tom's orientation to heroism, time, and everything else patriarchy stands for. Huck's heroics, on the other hand, are completely invisible. No one, not even Jim, knows what he went through to arrive at the decision to free Jim, yet what he has done makes him one of literature's greatest heroes. T. S. Eliot calls Huck "one of the permanent symbolic figures of fiction; not unworthy to take a place with Ulysses, Faust, Don Quixote, Don Juan, [and] Hamlet. . . ."[26] Odysseus and Huck can be placed together as heroes of the sacred feminine who work with the heroics of relationship, nature, and the heart. Huck disappears into the Territory at the end of the novel, with no trophy to show for his efforts. What remains is a great story told in his unique voice.

Personal Commentary

Huckleberry Finn is a much maligned book. It is widely although superficially known about, yet rarely *read.* It is a book many people think they have read, but haven't. They think they've read it, because they've seen film versions or plays based on it or they've heard of it. Perhaps they read it as children, but often it is confused with *Tom Sawyer.* The book is venerated as a kind of cultural icon, which is one way the patriarchal culture dilutes the book's profound criticism of that culture. By venerating a book, we don't have to read it.

When I was ten, my grandmother gave me a boxed set of *Tom Sawyer* and *Huckleberry Finn,* illustrated by Norman Rockwell. The folksy-sweet illustrations and the fact that my grandmother had taped a dollar on the frontispiece of each volume kept me from reading either book for years. It was enough just to own and display such an icon of culture! Luckily, somewhere along the way I did read *Huckleberry Finn.* I loved it, and it has become one of the books I *live* with. To me, Huck is real; he lives. I have an evolving relationship with him. Given this, I refuse to see any Huck Finn films or plays. I don't really like any of the illustrated editions, because I dislike the way he is made to be a cute rural-folksy, domesticated kid. This image is a denial of his dark side, his position as an outsider, his unkempt appearance, and his alienation. In *Tom Sawyer*, Twain says that "Huckleberry was cordially hated and dreaded by all the mothers of the town, because he was idle and lawless and vulgar and bad."[27]

The next time you see a kid hitchhiking, with long, straggly hair, clothes that have been slept in, and all his possessions in a backpack without a designer label, who looks ever so slightly *dangerous*, the kind of kid you probably wouldn't *think* of stopping to pick up—remember Huck Finn. You and I just passed him by on the highway.

Twain didn't make him adorable; we did. Twain didn't give him bib overalls with one suspender buckle undone, one front tooth missing, a straw hat, and freckles; we did. Twain gave us a boy who helped free a "nigger," who loved the "nigger" and traveled with him down the Mississippi River at night not wearing any clothes at all. Twain gave us a runaway, a boy who must stage his own death (and can't even tell his good friend Tom Sawyer) in order to be reborn, reconstruct his identity, and get as far away from us as possible. Perhaps he represents what Jungians call our Shadow; a dark, messy, uncontrolled, estranged part of us, a part we try to forget or sanitize into iconic cuteness. But if we read his story, he lives in us, haunting us with his example of heart-inspired morality and courage and with a sense that he left us and the patriarchy behind long ago. He lives in the wilderness of ourselves, but to find him we have to read his story, the one *he* wrote. At the end of the story Huck tells us quite plainly "what a trouble it was to make a book," so we can be quite certain he didn't illustrate it.

[1] Nor Hall, *The Moon and the Virgin: Reflections on the Archetypal Feminine* (New York: Harper & Row, 1980), p. 8.

[2] *Ibid.*

[3] Mark Twain, *The Adventures of Tom Sawyer* (Avon, CT: Heritage Press, 1964), p. 64.

[4] Starhawk, *The Spiral Dance* (San Francisco, CA: Harper & Row, 1979), pp. 2–3.

[5] Edward Whitmont, *The Return of the Goddess* (New York: Crossroad, 1982), p. 211.

[6] Whitmont, pp. 221, 222, 223.

[7] Mark Twain, *The Adventures of Huckleberry Finn* (Boston: Houghton Mifflin, 1958), p. 4. This text is cited hereafter, and all page numbers are in parentheses.

[8] In his famous essay on this book, T. S. Eliot calls the river a "God," but I think he should have called it a goddess, given that "the power and terror of Nature" is another way of speaking of the dual aspect of the Goddess as a creator and destroyer of life. "Water, like earth, has always been recognized in the human psyche as a feminine element" (J. Hawkes, *Dawn of the Gods*, London, 1968).

[9] Daniel G. Hoffman, "Black Magic—and White—in *Huckleberry Finn*," from *Adventures of Huckleberry Finn, A Norton Critical Edition* (W.W. Norton, 1962), p. 399.

[10] Hoffman, p. 400.

[11] Hoffman, p. 401.

[12] *Ibid.*

[13] Ann Belford Ulanov, *The Feminine* (Evanston, IL: Northwestern University Press, 1971), p. 326.

[14] Mark Twain, *Life on the Mississippi* (New York: New American Library, 1961), pp. 66–67.

[15] Ibid., p. 68.

[16] Ulanov, p. 183.

[17] Erich Neumann, "On the Moon and Matriarchal Consciousness," *Dynamic Aspects of the Psyche* (New York: The Analytical Psychology Club, 1956), p. 50.

[18] M. Esther Harding, *Woman's Mysteries, Ancient and Modern* (New York: Harper & Row, 1971), p. 96.

[19] *Ibid.*, p. 25.

[20] It is no accident that in the very next scene, the duke and the king dress Jim up to make him look like King Lear so they can leave him on the raft during the day and no one will think he's a runaway slave. In Shakespeare's famous tragedy (one of Twain's favorites), the education of Lear's heart begins with his dramatic mistreatment of his daughter Cordelia.

[21] "Lonesome" appears in the novel sixteen times, by my count.

[22] "Latin *provideo* meant 'to foresee;' *Providentia* meant divinatory magic. It was a personification of female prophetic or mantic talents, the quality that enabled ancient matriarchs to 'provide' for their dependents through foreknowledge of the stars and seasons, agriculture and food storage. In Christian usage, Providence was sometimes a synonym for God; but many mystics defined Providence as a female deity." Barbara G. Walker, *The Woman's Encyclopedia of Myths and Secrets* (New York: Harper & Row, 1983), p. 826.

[23] "Unlike Tom Sawyer, Huck does not flee the 'underground man' [Jim]; he joins him." Kenneth S. Lynn, "You Can't Go Home Again," from *Adventures of Huckleberry Finn, A Norton Critical Edition* (New York: W.W. Norton, 1962), p. 434.

[24] Jean Shinoda Bolen, "The Feminine Emerging," *Yoga Journal*, Jan./Feb 1988, p. 39.

[25] T. S. Eliot, "An Introduction to *Huckleberry Finn*," in *Adventures of Huckleberry Finn, A Norton Critical Edition* (New York: W.W. Norton, 1962), p. 327.

[26] *Ibid.*, p. 322.

[27] Mark Twain, *The Adventures of Tom Sawyer* (Avon, CT: Heritage Press, 1964), p. 61.

5

Macbeth

The most beautiful thing we can experience is the mysterious. It is the source of all true art and science. He to whom this emotion is a stranger, who can no longer pause to wonder and stand rapt in awe, is as good as dead: his eyes are closed.

—*Albert Einstein*

Shakespeare's play (1605) presents us with the story of a man and wife who kill Duncan, their beloved king, and assume his throne for the sake of power and ambition. Before they do this, Macbeth has an encounter with three magical women, whom he calls the Weird Sisters. They speak to him as "King hereafter," which leads him to mistake their prediction for a kind of otherworldly endorsement of his plans. Immediately after murdering Duncan, Macbeth and Lady Macbeth's lives begin to unravel. To stem the nightmarish tide running against him, Macbeth murders again and again. When he consults the Weird Sisters once more, they present him with images filled with ambiguities. Macbeth again fails to apprehend the full range of possible meanings inherent in utterances from such magical sources and hears only the meanings that serve his purposes. Just before his death, he draws the false conclusion that since his life has turned out to have no meaning, life itself is meaningless.

Macbeth is a terror-filled tragedy reflecting what happens when we lose harmony with ourselves, our hearts, and our allegiances, with time, Nature, and the Cosmos. Macbeth and Lady Macbeth act against every sign, law, custom, and sacred impulse from within. In their rush toward fame and ambition, they meet an ultimately death. *Macbeth* is Shakespeare's great denunciation of the worst excesses of the male values of ambition, the lust for power, and self-veneration. The play deals directly and concretely with issues of gender, both biological and, by implication, the larger philosophical connections to the masculine and feminine as principles.

The essence of the feminine principle is harmony, relationship, and the ability to find the connections between things.[1] The feminine valorizes harmony with the whole self, conscious and unconscious. It seeks harmony with others, acting not for itself alone, but in concert within the "web," the context of others, and in harmony with Nature, the largest context of all.[2] Because the feminine regards the self, others, and the world as engaged in a dialogue, it seeks an exchange from one depth to another, rather than relying on the simple mechanics of manipulation. This places great stress on *kairos* rather than *chronos*, on a careful, patient approach to time rather than a view of time as simply an opportunity. If I seek to act deeply, in concert with myself, others, and Nature, I must proceed slowly and meditatively in order to hear the voices of that context in the continuous series of inner and outer dialogues which is my life. This is why Ann Ulanov speaks of the "feminine style of attention . . . [as] a kind of contemplation; a dwelling upon the other"[3] and notes the importance of the "development of the feminine modality of understanding through pondering and waiting."[4] The feminine is not about passivity; it is about *timing* and waiting to take appropriate action.

In her articles on Taoism, the *Tao Teh Ching*, and the Goddess, Merlin Stone connects all three in the "*gentle omnipotence* of She who is the essence of the patterns of the universe, all that is actually implied when we speak of Mother Nature, that appears to be the core of the wisdom and the way of the *Tao Teh Ching*."[5] "Gentle omnipotence" is, of course, a paradox, and paradox is also one of the aspects of the feminine. Stone's example of gentle omnipotence is one offered by the *Tao Teh Ching* itself when it speaks of water: "The wisdom of the activity of the water flowing around a great boulder, rather than repeatedly crashing against it, is the wisdom of Mother Nature."[6] In another relevant verse, the Tao is described this way:

> The highest good is like water.
> Water gives life to the ten thousand things and does not strive.
> It flows in places men reject and so is like the Tao.
>
> In dwelling, be close to the land.
> In meditation, go deep in the heart.
> In dealing with others, be gentle and kind.
> In speech, be true.
> In ruling, be just.
> In business, be competent.
> In action, watch the timing.
>
> No fight: No blame.[7]

It is this wisdom and power of the feminine that is completely lost on Macbeth and Lady Macbeth, who will have little or nothing to do with humility, patience, receptivity, and the way of the feminine that involves a *dialogue* with reality. Their way is an apotheosis of the furthest excesses of male aggression, ambition, and haste. The *Tao Teh Ching* says: "The world is a sacred vessel, which must not be tampered with or grabbed after. To tamper with it is to spoil it, and to grasp it is to lose it. In fact, for all things there is a time for going ahead, and a time for following behind."[8]

The essence of the *Tao Teh Ching* is feminine in its veneration of Mother Nature and the Tao, or way of being in harmony with Nature, others, and oneself. The essence of *Macbeth* is the calamity that results when actions are taken in the name of pure will and selfish ambition, the very opposite of actions in harmony with the feminine, both as a gender and a principle. To understand how this violation occurs in *Macbeth*, we must begin with the three witches.

In the relatively short dramatic poem which is *Macbeth*, the figures who speak and embody the metaphoric are the three witches, Hecate's handmaidens.[9] These three "wyrd sisters" use metaphor even as they instruct Macbeth and the audience about the nature of metaphor. They are traditionally seen as forces of evil, when it would be more appropriate to think of them as Banquo does, as "instruments of darkness tell[ing] us truths."[10] Whether they tell us these truths to "win us to our harm," as

Banquo surmises, or to *warn* of our harm to ourselves is the crucial issue of the play. I contend that properly understood and read, prophecies from such immortal spirits are always paradoxical, and two-edged because prophecy stems from the realm of the metaphoric rather than the literal.[11] Macbeth tells his wife: "They have more in them than mortal knowledge" (I.v.2–3).

In Act One, Scene One, the witches chant in unison: "Fair is foul, and foul is fair," and I think this line is key to understanding the moral teaching of the play. This famous line is sometimes called the motto of the play, and it is also a gnomic way of depicting the nature of paradox. "Fair is foul, and foul is fair" is a metaphoric depiction of the truth Macbeth states more starkly two scenes later: "Nothing is / But what is not" (I.3.141–2). In essence, the three goddesses are saying that everything contains within it its opposite, that nothing is fixed, stable, one-sided, or one dimensional. What seems fair, or positive, is also foul, or negative. What seems foul, or dark, is also fair, or enlightening. At the heart of this metaphor is a poetic world view, a view of the world as flowing, ever-changing, always potentially more than what we know, more than what we theorize or would like to think.

William Blake was deeply committed to the paradoxical, what he called "the marriage of Heaven and Hell," and he put the vision of multiplicity inherent in paradox this way:

> Now I a fourfold vision see,
> And a fourfold vision is given to me;
> 'Tis fourfold in my supreme delight
> And threefold in soft Beulah's night
> And *twofold always. May God us keep*
> *From Single vision and Newton's sleep!*[12]

And in the *Tao Teh Ching* we find these lines that strongly echo the wisdom of the Weird Sisters:

> Bad fortune is what good fortune leans on,
> Good fortune is what bad fortune hides in.
> . . .
> What is normal soon becomes abnormal,
> And what is auspicious soon turns ominous.[13]

> Indeed, truth sounds like its opposite![14]

The witches, "these instruments of darkness," who have "beards" (I.3.46), these "secret, black, and midnight hags" (IV.1.48) bear complex truths for Macbeth from the paradoxical realm of the dark feminine. Macbeth is a military man, a man of action "disdaining Fortune" (I.2.19). His confrontation with them is a confrontation with his opposite, with feminine consciousness.

In opposition to the feminine and its knowledge of change and cyclicity is the viewpoint that reality should be stable, fixed, and constant. It is clearly a patriarchal world view based on control, reason, and order. It is significant that immediately after the three witches have vanished in Act One, Scene One, Duncan, the king of Scotland, enters and one of his captains describes "Fortune [as] a rebel's whore" (I.2.16,17). The notion that Fortune, or Fate, is a whore because she is "fickle"[15] derives from a patriarchal orientation toward existence, implying that if she were constant and true, Fortune would be faithful. The male wish to control fate, and thus reality, is strongly emphasized here. The play is positively riddled with references to men, maleness, manhood, male children, and manliness.[16] *Macbeth* is a play about the male principle in conflict with the feminine principle. The male principle is represented by Macbeth, and Lady Macbeth (after she has "unsexed" herself), as they struggle to advance their ambition and lust for power. The feminine principle is represented in the play by the three witches and their ambiguous advice and prophecy. They confront Macbeth with feminine wisdom, with what Elizabeth Sewell refers to as the orphic, poetic nature of life.[17]

In their first and most portentous appearance, they offer Macbeth and Banquo "strange intelligence" and greet him three times, as, "Thane of Glamis . . . Thane of Cawdor . . . [and] King hereafter" (I.3.50-55). The first he knows himself to be, the second has been newly bestowed by the King, which Macbeth doesn't yet know, and the third is something he secretly desires. Banquo asks why Macbeth starts and seems "to fear / Things that do sound so fair?" (I.3.56). Macbeth is profoundly shaken, because these women know his mind. Before Macbeth and Banquo speak, the three figures put their fingers to their lips to silence them as if to indicate they already know what the two men would ask. Later in the play, when Macbeth is presented with an apparition of an Armed Head conjured by the witches, one of the Sisters again silences his question for the vision: "He knows thy thought: Hear his speech but say thou naught" (IV.1.69-70). Nor Hall points out in *The Moon and the Virgin* that goddesses were often represented without mouths "perhaps because of the essential value of silence in feminine mysteries," and that "there is [a] kind of silence that is part of encountering the holy."[18]

Soon Macbeth learns that by an act of the king, he is no longer Thane of Glamis but has been made Thane of Cawdor,[19] and he naturally assumes that their prophecy of "King hereafter" is his true destiny as well. Macbeth wrestles with what he has heard from the witches with what has transpired to fulfill their words, and with his ambition and longing to become King. The Weird Sisters have cast upon Macbeth a dark riddle, a prophetic hieroglyphic snare; he struggles inside it trying to understand its meaning and discover what action to take. The riddle is not simply a puzzle to solve by intellectual adroitness; it is a living paradox Macbeth must confront and work through in his life and his decisions. Macbeth reflects on this paradox in a state of shock: "This supernatural soliciting / Cannot be ill; cannot be good. . . . My thought . . . shakes so my single state of man that function / Is smothered in surmise and nothing is / But what is not" (I.3.144–5; 152–56).

The witches' words have set in motion inside Macbeth "suggestion(s)," "image(s)," "fears," "imaginings," "thought(s)," which so shake his "*single state of man*" (italics mine) that his usual powers of direct and decisive action are overwhelmed by possibilities. For one brief moment in the play, Macbeth understands that this living paradox is not to be solved; it is to be lived and endured. For one moment Macbeth attains a glimmering of feminine wisdom when he muses to himself, "If chance will have me King, why chance / may crown me / Without my stir" (I.3.143–45).[20] This is feminine wisdom because it answers the witches' prophecy in kind. They, after all, said nothing to Macbeth about what he should or shouldn't do; they merely greeted him reflecting the past (Glamis), the present (Cawdor), and the future (King hereafter). His promotion, his move from Glamis to Cawdor, takes place without his planning and willing it; Chance (or Fate) brings him that rank. Moreover, the witches never speak of when or how he is to become King. In saying he will let Chance crown him, he is honoring both the way he became Thane of Cawdor and the mystery of how he might be "King hereafter." He did not stir to become Cawdor; so he will not stir to become King.

When Macbeth, still speaking to himself, adds: "Come what come may, / Time and the hour runs through the roughest day" (I.3.147–8), he is at his most receptive to time and paradox. For this one moment Macbeth grasps the import of the Weird Sisters. He is living with paradox, mystery, and reality and not exerting his will over it. When he next speaks, he explains his distraction to others by saying, "My dull brain was wrought / With things forgotten" (I.3.149–50). The things forgotten include an old wisdom of waiting, being patient, and allowing the paradoxes of reality to unfold on their own.

Thus far, Macbeth has met the three dark goddesses on their terms, and they have stimulated some of his murderous thoughts: "My thought, whose murder yet is but fantastical . . ." (I.3.139). The Weird Sisters (who are never called witches by either Macbeth or Banquo) have said nothing at all about murder, for that is not their mission. Their mission is to awaken Macbeth to his own inner depths and multiple dimensions. Their purpose is to shake his "single state of man" and to have him fully acknowledge his inner depths.

The weird sisters are oracular figures. Their words represent a kind of sacred text Macbeth calls "prophetic greeting" and "strange intelligence" (I.3.78,76). Lynda Sexson notes, "A sacred text is a means of divining one's inner self and one's relationship to the world of meaning. A sacred text reveals to us our identity, interpreting our present and calling up our future all in terms of our past. . . ."[21]

In Gilbert Murray's *Five Stages of Greek Religion,* he points out that when in the presence of an oracle, one didn't "ask questions of fact," one wanted "to know how . . . to behave."[22] Like all experiences of the numinous, one didn't treat the oracle as a mere dispenser of information, one approached a sacred oracle by entering into a true dialogue with its answers. The answers were usually poetic and metaphorical and required further reflection. Mircea Eliade makes the same point in his articles on the Delphic Oracle and the concept of Divination. At Delphi "the oracle . . . functioned as a sounding board."[23] He points out that:

> ". . . divination requires the radical submission of the diviner and
> indeed the client to the transcendental sources of truth, before their
> lives can be transformed, and set straight, before they can be
> reincorporated harmoniously into the world. Wisdom divination also
> often works . . . by freeing the inquirer from customary ways of
> thought. . . . One learns to see behind appearances and to cultivate a

continual attitude of tranquil self-offering. The very vagueness of the
answers in most forms of wisdom divination aid in this personal
appropriation, *making the client participate in shaping meaning out of
the session.*"[24] (Italics mine.)

This last notion is the key: the one who has the encounter with
some aspect of the divine *participates in shaping meaning* from the
encounter. This is exactly what Macbeth starts to do with his "If
chance will have me King. . . ." He begins a *dialogue* with the
prophecy of the Weird Sisters, and he and Banquo agree to ponder
their encounter with the three Sisters and discuss it later: "Think
upon what hath chanced, and at more time, / The interim having
weighed it, let us speak / Our free hearts to each other" (I.3.153–4).
Macbeth and Banquo have had a disturbing, complex encounter
with what Rudolf Otto calls the *numinous* and Mircea Eliade terms
hierophany, or a manifestation of the sacred.[25] As Eliade puts it, "one
must always reckon with the fact that the sacred discloses itself
under many modalities and upon different levels."[26] Macbeth's
"single state of man" is shaken by the encounter, and he speaks of a
whole range of inner responses, the internal dimensions of himself
in all their multiplicity: suggestions, images, fears, imaginings,
thoughts, surmises, his own brain, and his heart.

Macbeth's insight into this feminine realm is tenuous, and, unfor-
tunately, Lady Macbeth has not had a hierophanic encounter with the
three Sisters. She is not troubled by ambiguities or multiple possibilities. Lady Macbeth is caught up in a single-minded obsession with
ambition. In this sense she reminds me of what Sylvia Perera has written about certain successful women in a patriarchal culture.

'Daughters of the father'—that is, [women] well adapted to a
masculine-oriented society . . . have repudiated [their] own full
feminine instincts and energy patterns, just as the culture has
maimed or derogated most of them. . . . The patriarchal ego of both
men and women, to earn its instinct-disciplining, striving, progres-
sive, and heroic stance, has fled from the full-scale awe of the
goddess. Or it has tried to slay her, or at least to dismember and thus
depotentiate her.[27]

This description is strikingly apt for Lady Macbeth. When she gets her husband's letter about his encounter with the Weird Sisters, she never pauses for a moment to reflect on the possibilities for *awe* in the encounter he depicts: "When I burned in desire to question them further, they made themselves air, into which they vanished" (I.5.3–4). Macbeth goes on to say that he "stood rapt in the wonder of it," but Lady Macbeth's only wonder is whether Macbeth is not "too full o' th' milk of human kindness / To catch the nearest way" (I.5.15–16). From that moment on, her whole orientation takes a "heroic stance" and begins the process of dismembering the goddess in herself: "Unsex me here. . . . Come to my woman's breasts / And take my milk for gall" (I.5.17–18). What was for Macbeth a numinous, sacred encounter that reverberated inside him simply adds fuel to Lady Macbeth's ambitions for them both. She wants Macbeth to give up his newly discovered awareness of ambiguity and return to his "single state of man." When she asks "Art thou afeard / To be the same in thine own act and valor / As thou art in desire?" (I.7.39–41) she plays on Macbeth's desire to be king, completely ignoring his desire to honor and serve Duncan, who has been such a good king that "his virtues / Will plead like angels, trumpet-tongued against / The deep damnation of his taking-off" (I.7.18–20). Lady Macbeth manipulates Macbeth with one of the oldest fallacies at the heart of the patriarchy, namely that to be a man means to be single-minded and one dimensional, ignoring one's inner plurality and multifaceted consciousness. She would have Macbeth focus his masculinity exclusively on his ambition and his desire to become King and ignore his feelings of loyalty to Duncan and his feelings of affection for his King. After Macbeth meets the Weird Sisters, he begins to explore his own multiplicities and the many possibilities inherent in the world. Lady Macbeth, who has not had this divine encounter, draws his attention back to the unilateral.

After Macbeth has acceded to his wife's plan and killed the King, they cling to the single-mindedness that led to the murder:

> Lady Macbeth: These deeds must not be thought
> After these ways; so, it will make us mad. (II.2.33–4)

> Macbeth: To know my deed, 'twere best not know myself. (II.2.72)

> Macbeth: From this moment / The very firstlings of my heart shall be
> The firstlings of my hand. (IV.1.146-8)

Moments after Macbeth has actually killed Duncan, he reports hearing a voice: "Methought I heard a voice cry 'Sleep no more! / Macbeth does murder sleep'" (II.2.34–5). The voice may well be that of the Weird Sisters, for it goes on to call him by three names: "Still it cried 'Sleep no more!' to all the house; 'Glamis hath murdered sleep, and therefore Cawdor / Shall sleep no more, Macbeth shall sleep no more'" (II.2.40–2). Lady Macbeth equates manliness with not letting oneself think about such things as she tells her husband, "Why, worthy Thane, / You do unbend your noble strength to think / So brainsickly of things" (II.2.43–5). Macbeth and Lady Macbeth are unable to close their minds to what they have done. Lady Macbeth puts it fatuously: "A little water clears us of this deed. / How easy is it then!" (II.2.66–7). The harder they strive to maintain the "single state of man," the more they become engulfed in multiplicity. At the end, they both come unravelled. Lady Macbeth goes insane and commits suicide; Macbeth becomes a mass murderer before he is killed by Macduff and his army.

The tragedy of *Macbeth* lies in the conflict between the complex, multilayered nature of human consciousness and efforts to manipulate, control, and reduce that consciousness. The Weird Sisters' "strange intelligence" provokes a whole range of responses within Macbeth. In opposition to these "instruments of darkness [who] tell us truths" (I.3.124) are Lady Macbeth and Macbeth himself as they seek to steel themselves to a single task, to "screw [their] courage to the sticking place" (I.7.60) and overcome the implications of "the horrid deed" by willing themselves *not to think or feel*. In the name of ambition, Macbeth and his wife seek what she calls "the ornament of life" (i.e., the crown) (I.7.42). Macbeth's pursuit of this trophy is in opposition to his experience of the sacred. Faced with a choice between the dark truths of feminine consciousness embodied in the prophecies of the witches and the "ornament of life," to be achieved, ironically, by murder, Macbeth chooses the latter. Listen to what he says in Act 3, scene 4:

> Then comes my fit again. I had else been perfect;
> Whole as the marble, founded as the rock,
> As broad and general as the casing air.
> But now I am cabined, cribbed, confined, bound in
> To saucy doubts and fears. (III.4.21-25)

The language is rich with the conflict between the feminine realm of feelings (my fit, saucy doubts and fears) and patriarchal efforts to contain and deny them (perfect, marble, rock, cabined, cribbed, confined, bound). Marion Woodman offers an interesting and highly relevant commentary on this conflict and, in particular, on Macbeth's word "perfect":

> The goal-oriented, rational, perfectionist, masculine principle has to
> be balanced by the feminine. Our society has murdered the Great
> Mother, the inner life that feeds the spirit. . . . No other era has so
> totally divorced outer reality from inner reality, the matrix of which is
> the Great Mother. Never before have we been so cut off from the
> wisdom of nature and the wisdom of our instincts. What do we have
> left? The goddess at the center of our culture is the negative mother,
> one who would dash her baby's brains out and sacrifice love to
> power. She is Shakespeare's Lady Macbeth.[28]

Lady Macbeth and Macbeth divorce outer reality from inner, and turn reality, with its rich pluralistic possibilities for meaning into a narrow, one-dimensional blueprint for personal ambition. In this conflict between two different kinds of consciousness lies the essence of the tragedy. The Weird Sisters have everything to do with the feminine consciousness that opposes the ambition and power of the patriarchal value system.

One way to highlight the importance of the Weird Sisters is to think what the play would be like without them. Without them it would not be a tragedy; it would simply be a play about a *coup d'etat,* a military takeover. We read about them and no one dignifies them by calling them great tragedies. *Macbeth* is a great tragedy because there is so much at stake and so much is lost so quickly. Macbeth's tragedy is not that he kills Duncan—that is treasonous murder, not tragedy—but that in killing Duncan he also kills meaning. The Weird Sisters appear to enlighten Macbeth about the many facets of his identity, the many possibilities inherent in who Macbeth is, was, and could be. On the walls of the Delphic oracle were the words: "Know Thyself." The self is the *locus classicus* of all oracular encounters. How ironic that immediately after Macbeth has killed Duncan, he says, "To know my deed, 'twere best *not know myself*" (II.2.72; italics mine). The great tragedy here is that in the quest to gain more power, Macbeth has really shut down so much power in himself. In the act of gaining the crown, Macbeth gives up self-knowledge and the great gift of sleep: "great nature's second course,/ Chief nourisher in life's feast" (II.2.238–9). In the name of male power, Macbeth goes from thinking of life as a feast to his famous final soliloquy in which "Life's but a walking shadow . . ." (V.5.24).

Before that final moment arrives, in one last, desperate effort of will, Macbeth calls upon the Weird Sisters in Act 4, Scene 3 to determine what to do next, how to control the damage he has caused, or what new damage to inflict: "I am in blood / Stepped in so far that, should I wade no more, / Returning were as tedious as go o'er" (III.4.136–8). It is a scene full of powerful metaphors presented as a supernatural masque inside the dark cave of the Weird Sisters.[29] They show Macbeth three apparitions, called "masters" by the witches: "Say if th' hadst rather hear it from our mouths / Or from our masters" (IV.1.63). This clearly establishes the Weird Sisters' allegiance with the realm of magic, where the imagination and the multiple possibilities of the metaphoric meet in what Neumann calls matriarchal consciousness. The apparitions, like the Weird Sisters themselves in Act One, bring what Cleanth Brooks names as "the paradox that will destroy the overbrittle rationalism on which Macbeth founds his career."[30] Once again, Macbeth is confronted with the task of divination, with weighing the ambiguous possibilities of the numinous and creating a dialogue, and again he opts for the literal.

The first apparition is an Armed Head that brings knowledge Macbeth already knows: to fear Macduff. The second apparition, a Bloody Child, confuses the information of the first by saying, "none of woman born / Shall harm Macbeth" (IV.1.80–1). This would seem to make Macbeth invulnerable, for who is *not* of woman born? The third and last apparition is a Child Crowned, with a tree in his hand who informs Macbeth that he "shall never vanquished be until / Great Birnam Wood to high Dunsinane Hill / Shall come against him" (IV.1.92-3). Macbeth assumes "that will never be" (IV.1.94) and declares of all three apparitions: "Sweet bodements, good!" (IV.1.96). What he doesn't realize is that he has so alienated nature with his murder of Duncan that he succeeds in metaphorically calling up the archetype of the Green Man to set things right. When Malcolm orders his men to move against Macbeth's castle of Dunsinane, the men do so disguised with boughs from the trees of Birnam Wood.

One would have thought by now that he might have had second

thoughts about any information associated with the Weird Sisters. These three symbols are so ambiguous on the surface: why does the first image warn Macbeth to "beware Macduff" if the second and third images are correct and he is invulnerable? Only a few scenes earlier, Macbeth has said to Lady Macbeth, "Stones have been known to move and trees to speak" (III.4.123). Given this familiarity with supernatural possibilities, why he is so confident Birnam Wood will not come to Dunsinane? After all, if stones have been known to move—why not trees? Macbeth has already encountered the three Weird Sisters, seen a dagger before his eyes, and seen Banquo's ghost. All of this should have awed him sufficiently to give him pause, but such is not the case for Macbeth. He gives himself over all the more to impulsive action without reflection: "From this moment / The very firstlings of my heart shall be / The firstlings of my hand . . . be it thought and done" (IV.1.146–8,149). This speed and impulsiveness in the face of such profound images is a blatant denial of the power of the feminine as Neuman describes it:

> The ego of matriarchal consciousness is used to keeping still until the time is favorable, until the process is complete, until the fruit of the moon-tree has ripened into a full moon; that is, until comprehension has been born out of the unconscious. . . . It is in the act of "understanding" that the peculiar and specific difference between the processes of matriarchal and patriarchal consciousness first becomes apparent. For matriarchal consciousness, understanding is not an act of the intellect, functioning as an organ for *swift* registration, development and organization; rather, it has the meaning of a "conception." Whatever is to be understood must first "enter" matriarchal consciousness in the full, sexual, symbolic meaning of a fructification.[31]

In the dark cave of the Weird Sisters, the symbolic locus of the unconscious, Macbeth again fails to let his conception of these oracular images slowly grow to a birthing of their full, profound meanings. Neumann's idea could be used to describe Macbeth's dilemma at the words of the second apparition, "Laugh to scorn / The pow'r of man, for none of woman born / Shall harm Macbeth." Because he refuses to be born in the sense of the feminine consciousness he has encountered, Macbeth himself poses the danger. He should scorn the power of man and become the bloody child, born of this sacred, feminine consciousness. Because Macbeth won't allow it, he is the one who most harms himself. Macbeth refuses to allow himself to be "of woman born," and so brings ruin to himself and his entire country. Moments later we hear Ross speak to Macduff and Malcolm, who are in exile in England, about the state of Scotland: "Alas, poor country, / Almost afraid to know itself. It cannot / Be called *our mother* but our grave, where nothing / But who knows nothing is once seen to smile" (IV.3.164–7; italics mine).

In England, the king is the complete opposite of Macbeth. There, Edward the Confessor is able to heal people with his touch:

> With this strange virtue,
> He hath a h*eavenly gift of prophecy,*
> And sundry blessings hang about his throne
> That speak him full of grace. (IV.3.156–9; italics mine)

Before Macbeth's world comes completely apart, he delivers his famous last soliloquy in which he declares that "Life's but a walking shadow . . . it is a tale / Told by an idiot, full of sound and fury, / Signifying nothing" (V.5.24,26–8). Birnam Wood does come to Dunsinane, and Macbeth is killed by Macduff—who was delivered by Caesarian section and thus was not born at all. The crucial phrase in the soliloquy is "signifying nothing." It is the conclusion of someone who, after a short-lived engagement with meaning, set about to shut down the possibilities of meaning, and not know himself. Before he is slain, Macbeth curses the Weird Sisters, calling them "juggling fiends no more believed, / That palter with us in a double sense (V.7.19–20): and reveals that he has missed the point. Their point is the point of all prophetic, oracular metaphor, which is the language of feminine consciousness. That language is always framed at least "in a double sense" because it is about multiplicity and its inherent enormously rich range of possible meanings. Far from being "a tale. . . . Signifying nothing"; the dialogue with the sacred that the Weird Sisters initiate in Macbeth could have made his life a tale signifying *everything,* if he had only allowed meaning to be "of woman born."

Personal Commentary

It's hard to relate to or to comprehend Macbeth's bloody deeds. He kills his king and the king's two grooms with his own hands, and orders the murder of Banquo, Fleance, and Macduff's wife and children. That way lies madness. But it is not hard to understand his obsession with ambition and haste, or his runaway egotism. Were he alive today, he'd find himself very much at home in our get-yours-while-you-can ethos. Had we been in his shoes, many of us might well have used the numinous encounter with the Weird Sisters as fuel for personal self-interest.

If, in the future, few of us recognize the numinous in the form of a psychic encounter, a prophetic dream, a powerful synchronistic coincidence, or any other form, then this play will simply seem anachronistic and foolish to us. Until that time comes, the play is still relevant to our understanding of the labyrinthine ways of the feminine that our male-dominated culture ignores. We are all driven by linear, hierarchical values: more is better than less, faster is better than slower, and being famous for *any* reason is superior to everything. When we are brought face to face with the labyrinth of the feminine or a way of life involving paradox, slowness, silence, patience, and humility, most of us find we are as ill-prepared as Macbeth to respond appropriately. I certainly can't say I would have behaved much differently. What haunts me is that although I would not have become a murderer for ambition's sake, I might well have thought of other ways to inflate my self-importance because of a supernatural encounter. The temptation would be to see such an event as a kind of spiritual anointing of one's life and thereby let it greatly magnify the importance of that life and turn it into another kind of egotism.

I have had a few psychic encounters in my life and some striking synchronistic affirmations. I am trying to deal with them in the context of Macbeth's mistakes, i.e., to keep them in the private realm. William Butler Yeats, in an essay on magic, cautions against saying too much about such "hidden things":

> I have come to believe so many strange things because of experience
> that I see little reason to doubt the truth of many things that are
> beyond my experience; and it may be that there are beings who watch
> over that ancient secret, as all tradition affirms, and resent, and
> perhaps avenge, too fluent speech. They say in the Aran Islands that if
> you speak over-much of the things of Faery your tongue becomes like
> a stone.[32] (*Essays and Introductions,* New York: Collier Books,
> 1986, p. 51)

This passage reminds me that the Weird Sisters put their fingers to their lips three times urging Macbeth to keep silent. If he had kept what he saw, heard, and felt inside the silent labyrinth of himself instead of turning it into a platform for action, he would have properly venerated the Weird Sisters' dark, feminine wisdom, and it might have become his own.

---

[1] Nor Hall, *The Moon and the Virgin: Reflections on the Archetypal Feminine* (New York: Harper and Row, 1980), p. 8.

[2] Carol Gilligan, *In a Different Voice* (Cambridge, MA: Harvard University Press, 1983), p. 48 and *passim*.

[3] Ann Belford Ulanov, *The Feminine* (Evanston, IL: Northwestern University Press, 1971), p. 332.

[4] *Ibid.*, p. 328.

[5] Merlin Stone, *Ancient Mirrors of Womanhood* (Boston: Beacon Press, 1984), p. 25 (italics mine).

[6] *Ibid.*, p. 26.

[7] Lao Tsu, *Tao Te Ching*, translated by Gia-Fu Feng and Jane English (New York: Alfred A. Knopf, 1974), number 8.

[8] Lao Tzu, *Tao Teh Ching*, translated by Dr. John C. H. We (New York: St. John's University Press, 1961), number 29, p. 41.

[9] Act 3, Scene 5, the scene in which Hecate addresses the three witches, is often disputed as a later addition not by Shakespeare, but there is no dispute that the three are Hecate's agents.

[10] William Shakespeare, *The Tragedy of Macbeth*, ed. Alfred Harbage (Baltimore, MD: Penguin Books, 1956), I.3.137. This is the text used throughout.

[11] Katherine Briggs writes of the witches in *Macbeth*, "It is doubtful if they are human beings." (*Pale Hecate's Team: An Examination of the Beliefs on Witchcraft and Magic Among Shakespeare's Contemporaries and His Immediate Successors*, New York: The Humanities Press, 1962.)

[12] William Blake, *The Essential Blake*, ed. Stanley Kunitz (New York: Ecco Press, 1987), pp. 84–85.

[13] *Tao Teh Ching*, trans. John Wu, number 58, p. 83.

[14] *Ibid.*, number 78, p. 111.

[15] See the note to the Folger edition of *Macbeth* (editor Louis B. Wright, New York: Washington Square Press, 1959, p. 2).on "whore:" "The fickleness of the goddess Fortune was a proverbial idea which earned her the name of whore more than once in Elizabethan writings."

[16] I count at least twenty-eight such references.

[17] Elizabeth Sewall, *The Orphic Voice* (New Haven, CT: Yale University Press, 1960), p. 47

[18] Nor Hall, p. 59.

[19] Insofar as the former Thane of Cawdor turned out to be a traitor against the King, someone the King once thought of as "a gentleman on whom I built an absolute trust" (I.4.15), this part of the witches' prophecy alone should give Macbeth pause, pause to

reflect on the paradox, the ironic distinction of being named the *new* Thane of Cawdor.

20 This recalls Huck's learning to trust Providence.

21 Lynda Sexson, *Ordinarily Sacred* (New York: Crossroad, 1982), p. 29.

22 Gilbert Murray, *Five Stages of Greek Religion* (Garden City: Doubleday, 1955), p. 36

23 *The Encyclopedia of Religion*, vol. 4, ed. Mircea Eliade (New York: MacMillan), pp. 277–78.

24 *Ibid.*, p. 381.

25 Mircea Eliade, *Myths, Dreams, and Mysteries* (New York: Harper Torchbooks, 1975), pp. 124–25.

26 *Ibid.*, p. 130.

27 Sylvia Perera, *Descent to the Goddess* (Toronto: Inner City Books, 1981), p. 7.

28 Marion Woodman, *Addiction to Perfection* (Toronto: Inner City Books, 1982), pp. 13, 19, 20.

29 Many editions cite this as the set direction for the scene. The cave is a classic symbol of the dark feminine.

30 Cleanth Brooks, *The Well Wrought Urn* (New York: Harcourt Brace World, 1947), p.

31 Erich Neumann, "On the Moon and Matriarchal Consciousness," *Dynamic Aspects of the Psyche* (New York: The Analytical Psychology Club, 1956), p. 47 (italics mine).

32 William Butler Yeats, *Essays and Introductions* (New York: Collier Books, 1986), p. 51.

6

A Midsummer Night's Dream

Constancy itself is nothing but a languishing and wavering dance.

—Montaigne

Shakespeare's famous comedy A Midsummer Night's Dream *(1596) is about love and marriage and the Fairies' magical world of the forest. Six sets of couples have comic adventures that embody the play's action: Theseus and Hippolyta, Hermia and Lysander, Helena and Demetrius, Oberon and Titania (King and Queen of the Fairies), and Pyramus and Thisby. At the very center of the play are Bottom and Titania, and the dream Bottom has while sleeping in her arms. The woodland spirit Puck, trying to serve Oberon's wishes, creates matchings and mismatchings of several of these characters until the relationships are sorted out in the last act. At the play's close the Fairies bless the mortal couples and their forthcoming marriages.*

While in most major respects *Macbeth* and *A Midsummer Night's Dream*[1] could not be more different, at their centers both plays present ways of contacting the numinous and touching the web of sacred, symbolic reality.

One of Shakespeare's major sources for *Macbeth* was Raphael Holinshed's *The Chronicles of England, Scotland, and Ireland,* written in 1577. In Holinshed's published account of the historical Macbeth's meeting with the Weird Sisters, he describes the figures as "three women in strange and wild apparel, resembling creatures of elder world . . . either the weird sisters, that is (as ye would say) the goddesses of destiny, or else some nymphs or feiries."[2] Weird sisters, creatures of elder world, goddesses of destiny, nymphs, or "feiries" are multiple names approximating a multiple reality. These three beings are hard to pin down, hard to name or classify precisely, because they are supernatural figures. In Eliade's terms these numinous, hierophanic manifestations of the sacred are "The manifestation of something of a wholly different order, a reality that does not belong to our world. . . ."[3] Macbeth's precipitating failure occurs when he becomes profoundly ambivalent and turns disturbing knowledge from "the creatures of elder world" into a single-minded plan of action. What should have awed and made him humble, or at least given him metaphysical and personal reasons for pause, made him an impatient runaway killer. In the potentially rich dialogue he and Banquo are presented with what should have been an occasion for divination, a time that would allow him and Banquo to reflect on their experience, becomes an endorsement of Macbeth's personal ambition.

Because Macbeth fails to truly listen to the multiple layers of meaning inherent in the prophecy of these three "nymphs or feiries," he loses access to the whole of his inner life, his inner meaning—thus, symbolically, he even murders his own sleep. For Macbeth, his life ends as a meaningless "tale told by an idiot."

In *A Midsummer Night's Dream,* Bottom has a complex and profoundly mysterious encounter with the numinous. He spends the night sleeping and dreaming entwined in the arms of Titania, herself a "creature of elder world," a goddess, a manifestation of Diana,[4] a fairy—in this play, the Queen of the Fairies. The crucial feature of Bottom's response to the supernatural is that he is deeply changed by it; he is quieted by the encounter. He knows he has been given an extraordinary experience, one *so full* of meaning that he calls it "a most rare vision"

(IV.1.203). Unlike Macbeth, who murders sleep, Bottom not only sleeps but lies in the arms of a goddess and has a visionary dream, "a dream past the wit on man to say what dream it was. . . . It shall be called 'Bottom's Dream,' because it hath no bottom . . ." (IV.1.203–4;212–13). Given Bottom's response of reverence and humility, he might have described his life as a tale told by a foolish weaver, full of gentleness and mystery, signifying *everything!* But before we look at his encounter with Titania and her fairy retinue at the heart of *Dream,* we need to look at the play as a whole.

If Macbeth is about the poison of alienation, *Dream,* in its devotion to love and its many unions, is the antidote. The comedy opens with Theseus, King of Athens, and his bride-to-be, Hippolyta, discussing their nuptial plans. It ends with the royal couple joined by their subjects Hermia and Lysander and Demetrius and Helena, who all are anticipating their weddings. Once these mortals are off stage, the divine couple Oberon and Titania and their train of fairies dance and sing, blessing the human unions: "Hand in hand, with fairy grace, / Will we sing, and bless this place" (V.1.388–9). Shakespeare has filled his play with lovers seeking union (including the lovers Pyramus and Thisby in the play-within-the-play); *Dream* is his great dramatic depiction of *hierosgamos.* *Dream* celebrates marriage as a metaphor for a sacred union with one's beloved and with all of life.

It was a commonplace assumption in medieval and Renaissance thought that the entire universe was woven together like a giant tapestry, each thread contributing to and interacting with the whole in a divine pattern or order. In Shakespeare's day there were "certain fundamental assumptions which every thoughtful Elizabethan took for granted . . . [namely that] man is not something by himself; he is 'a piece of the order of things' . . . the knot and chain of nature; it is impossible to think of him apart from the rest of creation."[5] This order of things has been variously described as a "great chain of being"[6] or as a cosmic dance.[7] In Shakespeare's *Troilus and Cressida,* Ulysses delivers the famous speech on cosmic and human order, the interrelationship between the macrocosm and the microcosm, pointing out that "the *unity* and *married* calm of states" on earth can quickly be brought to chaos by disorder in the heavens and visa versa (I.3.100; italics mine). In *Cosmos and History,* Eliade suggests the proliferation of the metaphorical implications of the *hierosgamos* when he says "marriage rites . . . have a divine model, and human marriage reproduces the hierogamy, more especially the union of heaven and earth."[8] He further points out that the cosmic myth of hierogamy "serves as the exemplary model not only in the case of marriages but also in the case of any other ceremony whose end is the restoration of integral wholeness."[9]

Thus *Dream* presents us with marriage as a sacred union throughout the human and divine order. Ultimately the play is a celebration that ends in a May Day dance and seeks to restore this integral wholeness. The play, in fact, is about several different kinds of sacred union. In addition to the unions between its human and divine characters, the play is about the restoration of integral wholeness between patriarchal and feminine consciousness, as depicted by Egeus and his daughter Hermia, and between Theseus' own "cool reason" as an archetype of consciousness and the poetic imagination demonstrated by Bottom.

We never really fear that Egeus' claims of ownership, demand for obedience, and retribution to Hermia are going to amount to much, but these claims are, in fact, ugly, menacing, and serious enough to send Hermia and Lysander fleeing into the forest on May Day eve under a full moon, thereby setting the play in motion. Egeus refuses to allow his daughter to marry Lysander, insisting that by "the ancient privilege of Athens / As she is mine, I may dispose of her" (I.1.41–2). He orders her, on pain of death or exile, to follow his wishes and marry Demetrius. Theseus adds his support to this patriarchal code when he omits any reference to her mother, to the role of the feminine in creation, in his advice to Hermia:

> To you your father should be as a god,
> One that composed your beauties; yea, and one
> To whom you are but as a form in wax,
> By him imprinted, and within his power
> To leave the figure, or disfigure it. (I.1.47-51)

But neither Egeus nor Theseus is able to do more that threaten to use the power of Athenian law in this play, for it is an enchanted night, an evening when the real power belongs to the moon, the fairies, and the wood. Macbeth is given over to the masculine principle in actuality and rhetoric so we are not surprised to learn that within the play "the moon is down." *Dream* is all about restoring the balancing between masculine and feminine; the moon is full, and her spirit is ever-present. In the course of the play the moon is referred to, in one way or another, almost fifty times.

More important, the feminine forces inhabiting the moonlit woods outside of Athens are able to effect *inner* changes beneath the masculine outer imprinting of the "form in wax." According to the stated code of behavior, Egeus "should be as a god" to Hermia, but in her mind he is not. This is the classic conflict between the masculine principle of law and abstract consciousness and feminine consciousness and its acknowledgment of feeling and instinct. Hermia knows her feelings and her soul and refuses to succumb to a legal abstraction; her "soul consents not to give sovereignty" to her father's "unwished yoke" (I.1.83;82). She truly loves Lysander, and nothing will change that. She knows her heart. In Erich Neumann's terms, "the seat of matriarchal consciousness is in the heart and not the head . . . [and] the ego of patriarchal consciousness, our familiar head-ego often knows nothing of what goes on in the deeper center of consciousness in the heart."[10]

This is why the play takes place in the forest, *away* from the reach of patriarchal Athenian law. Deep in the heart of a moonlit forest where the various alignments and misalignments between the worlds of Oberon and Titania, Hermia and Lysander, and Helena and Demetrius take place and where "Jack shall have Jill, / Naught shall go ill" (III.3.461–2), is Bottom's encounter with Titania.

Bottom's response to his encounter is in stark contrast to the interrelationships of macrocosm and microcosm in *Macbeth*. When Macbeth acts selfishly, not as "a piece of the order of things," and violates the sacred order to kill Duncan, Nature's order is violated as well, and we learn that on the night of the murder a sparrow kills a hawk and horses fight and devour each other. In *Dream*, the *hierosgamos* is celebrated to end the quarreling between Oberon and Titania as the King and Queen of the Fairies. Their quarrel (over the possession of the changling boy) has created such a disturbance in Nature that the seasons themselves are disordered:

> The spring, the summer,
> The chiding autumn, angry winter change
> Their wonted liveries; and the mazed world,
> By their increase, now knows not which is which. (II.1.111-114)

As Titania puts it, a "progeny of evils comes / From our debate, from our dissension" (II.1.115–116). So about the middle of the play, as a result of the manipulations of both humans and the fairies, nearly everything and everyone is in a state of comic mismatch. Egeus and Hermia are estranged through an error on Puck's part that reflects the disharmony in the fairy realm. Lysander, Hermia, Demetrius, and Helena are in consternation, and Oberon and Titania are still at odds. In the midst of all this human and divine confusion, Bottom, with the head of an ass bestowed by Puck, has a magical encounter with Titania and her fairy retinue.

Bottom is the true hero of *Dream* because he is the play's great loving constant. Even though he has the head of an ass, he is essentially unaffected by Oberon and Puck's mischief. Because of their mischief, Titania loves Bottom until the spell is broken. Bottom seems the fool in appearing as an ass, but inside he is the same gentle, loving, empathetic, unassuming person he has always been. His divine encounter with Titania deepens him because in the encounter he makes authentic contact with Titania and all her mysteries. When Bottom meets Titania's fairy entourage, in his gracious and unassuming way he asks of Peaseblossom, Cobweb, Moth, and Mustardseed each fairy's name so that he may know them and have a conversation or dialogue with them. Bottom is completely natural and at home with the fairy world because his loving, accepting nature allows him to be. He is Nick Bottom, the weaver, and metaphorically he already has warp and weft of the ordinary and the numinous within him. He is already engaged in the business of his own inner *hierosgamos,* that complex interweaving of heaven and earth, and so he is able to accept this sacred encounter, on its own terms.

As Bottom and Titania fall asleep in one another's arms, she further underscores this image of union, of the sacred cloth they weave together, when she says to him:

> Sleep thou, and I will wind thee in my arms.
> . . .
> So doth the woodbine the sweet honeysuckle
> Gently entwist; the female ivy so
> Enrings the barky fingers of the elm.
> O, how I love thee! how I dote on thee! (IV.1.39–44)

Titania wakes, released from her spell, and dances away with Oberon. Their reconciliation is complete, and they leave Bottom to wake alone.

But when he wakes, Bottom remembers his experience fully; his famous soliloquy echoes the Old and the New Testaments as he reflects on the sacred nature of that experience. True to his unique consciousness, which accepts his unity with the sacred, he revealingly mixes up language from Isaiah and Corinthians[11] as he tries to speak of his rare vision:

> I have had a most rare vision. I have had a
> dream, past the wit of man to say what dream it
> was. . . . The eye of man hath not heard, the ear
> of man hath not seen, man's hand is not able to
> taste, his tongue to conceive, nor his heart to
> report what my dream was. I will get Peter Quince
> to write a ballet of this dream. It shall be
> called 'Bottom's Dream,' because it hath no bottom. . . .
> (IV.1.1203–5; 208–13)

Unlike Macbeth, who turns his hierophanic encounter into fuel for the single focus of his ambition, Bottom plans to make a song ("a ballet") out of his experience; the song will have many dimensions because the experience itself was multidimensional. In the next scene, Bottom is reunited with his friends Quince, Flute, Snout, and Starveling and struggles to tell them something of what has happened, vacillating between wanting to speak and not being able to:[12]

> Bottom: Masters, I am to discourse wonders; but ask me
> not what. For if I tell you, I am not true Athenian.
> I will tell you everything, right as it fell out.
>
> Quince: Let us hear, sweet Bottom.
>
> Bottom: Not a word of me. . . . No more words. Away, go, away!
> (IV.2.26–30;40)

And so Bottom does not make a ballad of his dream and is left in a kind of awe and silence, embodying the deep humility that underlies all encounters with the numinous. Nor Hall points out that silence ". . . is part of encountering the holy. When in the presence of something overwhelming, one is silenced by the magnitude of the experience. It is mysterious because it is ineffable—there are simply no words to explain."[13]

Immediately following Bottom's declaration of wordlessness about his experience, Theseus and Hippolyta appear. Theseus delivers a famous speech ridiculing "the lunatic, the lover, and the poet" for having seething brains, shaping fantasies, and imaginations that *misconstrue* the true nature of reality. Like a stand-in for Plato and the patriarchal consciousness of *The Republic,* Theseus implicitly praises "cool reason" for its stability over against the way "imagination bodies forth / The forms of things unknown" (V.1.4–15). This is all high irony on Shakespeare's part because Theseus has had no contact with "the forms of things unknown," and we have just witnessed Bottom's profound contact with such things. In mocking poets, Theseus ironically paraphrases the very essence of the *hierosgamos,* or the sacred marriage of heaven and earth:

> The poet's eye, in a fine frenzy rolling,
> Doth glance from heaven to earth, from earth to heaven; (V.1.12–13)

We might wish to say to Theseus what Hamlet said to Horatio, namely that "There are more things in heaven and earth, Horatio, / Than are dreamt of in your philosophy" (*Hamlet* I.5.166–67). But Bottom's dream and the play itself have already done the work of showing us wonders, multiplicities, and the reality of the "more things" than can be accounted for in a reductive philosophy.

When Theseus claims it is the tricks of the imagination that turn the unknown into shapes and "in the night, imagining some fear, / How easy is a bush supposed a bear!" (V.1.21–22), he is totally unaware of Puck! Puck is a shape-changer like other manifestations of the elder world—in name (Puck, Robin Goodfellow, Hobgoblin, mad spirit, etc.) and in deed. He tells us he can assume the likenesses of a filly foal, a roasted crab, a three-footed stool, a horse, a hound, a hog, a fire, and a headless bear (perhaps Theseus' "bush supposed a bear").[14] In this play the Green Man makes an obvious appearance in the form of Puck. I like to think of Bottom as an honorary Green Man, too, because he wears his animal head with acceptance and aplomb. Jeffrey Russell suggests that the hood worn by Robin Hood may have been an animal's head.[15] Indeed, Bottom and his ass-head are like a comedic Green Man or a fertility spirit who could be either "frightening or funny."

Throughout the play, reality is so complex it forms a vortex of multiplicities, and Theseus, King of Athens, and voice of reason, may be the only one who isn't aware of it. His bride-to-be, Hippolyta, is closer to the truth of the play when, in response to his speech deriding the imagination, she refers to the play's deepest truth, which has *grown* out of the story of the night. She speaks of Hermia, Lysander, Helena, and Demetrius, and by implication, Bottom, when she says:

> But the story of the night told over,
> And all their minds transfigured so together,
> More witnesseth than fancy's images
> And grows to something of great constancy;
> But howsoever, strange and admirable. (V.1.22–27)

Her words are true for the play as well. It is a story of the night about the transfiguration of mind, consciousness, and the realities that are "more . . . than fancy's images." This is the consciousness that has room for both reason ("something of great constancy") *and* the "strange and admirable." It seems appropriate that Hippolyta, Queen of the Amazons, should give such a rejoinder to Theseus's mocking speech. The line mixes fancy and constancy and the strange and the admirable. This blend of something of constancy and the strange and admirable creates the new mind of the play, with "minds transfigured so together" that they contain the *hierosgamos* itself.

Near the very end of *Dream,* Theseus thinks he has the last word as he commands everyone to bed. Like an autocrat who lives by the clock, he interrupts the final moments of *Pyramus and Thisby* to announce, "The iron tongue of midnight hath told twelve. / Lovers, to bed; 'tis almost fairy time" (V.1.352–3). These two lines summarize the two kinds of consciousness in the play, using both kinds of time as metaphors. There is *chronos,* the rationally ordered time told by the clock; and there is fairy time, which, in Ann Ulanov's terms, is *kairos,* or feminine time measured not by the clock, but by the living tongues of nature.[16] Puck gives us the reckoning of fairy time this way:

> Now the hungry lion roars,
> And the wolf behowls the moon;
> . . .
> Whilst the screech owl, screeching loud,
> . . .
> Now it is the time of night
> That the graves, all gaping wide,

> Every one lets forth his sprite,
> In the churchway paths to glide.
> As we fairies, that do run
> By the triple Hecate's team
> From the presence of the sun,
> Following darkness like a dream,
> Now are frolic. (V.1.360–1;365;368–376)

Theseus, as King of Athens, personifies the linear consciousness of reason in a form limited by the iron tongue of the clock. His reference to "fairy time" is rhetorical; he has no awareness that the moment he finishes his speech and retires to his room, the royal palace will fill with the music, singing, dancing and frolicking of Puck, Oberon, Titania, and the fairies. Unbeknownst to Theseus, fairy time is real, and the fairies themselves are real. Both are not governed by the law of the clock and the linear consciousness of the patriarchy; but as Puck says, "do run / By the triple Hecate's team," or by the goddess. As Madeleine Doran indicates in her textual notes to this edition, this is "Hecate in her three aspects as Luna in the sky, Diana on earth, [and] Proserpina in the underworld."[17] Fairy time is Shakespeare's way of talking about what Erich Neumann calls matriarchal consciousness. Herbert Marcuse refers to this form of consciousness as "transcendent" or "true consciousness" that is critical of the dominant order of things and still remembers the multidimensional universe.[18] It is a consciousness of more possibilities than are contained in the realm of the established order. This generous, loving, consecrating spirit is personified by Titania, as she extends her magical blessing throughout the house to every sleeping couple:

> First rehearse your song by rote,
> To each word a warbling note.
> Hand in hand, with fairy grace,
> Will we sing, and bless this place. (V.1.386–90)

When all is said and done, *A Midsummer Night's Dream* is aptly named after a specific dream and not a particular character, because it is more about consciousness than it is about any one individual. We may mix up the names of the lovers (Hermia and Lysander, Helena and Demetrius) or fail to recall Theseus' or Egeus' roles in the plot, but no one can forget Bottom the fool with the head of an ass, who shares a transforming night of love with the goddess Titania, a descendant of the Titans—the progeny of the great Goddess Gaia. This is a play about the moon, magic, metamorphosis, and the mingling of humans with the elder world of spirits. It doesn't seem too far-fetched to think of Bottom as a kind of comedic shaman or shape-changer, and his wearing of the ass-head as a mask, or second head as symbolic of integral conscious-ness that encompasses the animal world of nature.[19] Only a very wise fool could be so at home in *both* his human and animal nature. Only a very wise fool could make love with the Goddess.

Personal Commentary

Structurally, *A Midsummer Night's Dream* is like a nest of Chinese boxes: you open the lid and find another box inside, open it and find another, and so on. The boxes here are the relationships in the play: Theseus and Hippolyta; the lovers Hermia and Lysander, Helena and Demetrius; Oberon and Titania from the realm of the Faery; and finally in the play-within-the-play, the characters Pyramus and Thisby. Then there's Bottom, with the head of an ass, making love to Titania under the spell of her enchanted love for him. When Bottom awakes and de-livers his soliloquy, he speaks of having had a dream, a most rare vision. Does he mean the whole dreamlike experience of meeting Titania and her fairy train before they fell asleep? Or does he mean the *very dream* he had while he spent the night with her? I think he means both, but what I love most about this dreamlike play is that at its very heart is a *second* "Bottom's dream," an actual dream he has while he sleeps in the arms of the Queen of the Fairies. It is about this secret dream that he can't speak and must keep silent.

Among all of the nested boxes, the last is this mysterious box Bot-tom leaves unopened. Then perhaps we should add to our list of rela-tionships Bottom and his dream. It is a gift from the goddess, which, no doubt, contains another set of boxes; but we'll never know. Like the great comic Magus he is, Bottom says of his experience: "No more words." Still I love to imagine what is in that mysterious 'Bottom-less' dream at the deep center of the play.

[1] William Shakespeare, *A Midsummer Night's Dream*, ed., Madeleine Doran (Baltimore, MD: Penguin Books, 1967). This is the text used throughout, henceforth referred to as *Dream*.

[2] G. Blakemore Evans, ed.,*The Riverside Shakespeare* (Boston: Houghton Mifflin Co., 1974), p. 1342.

[3] Mircea Eliade, *The Sacred and the Profane* (New York: Harcourt, Brace & World, 1959), p. 11.

[4] "The goddess Diana or Artemis of classical lore appears to have been particularly identified with the fairy tradition. . . . Diana, at a later time, became the leader and protectress of the mediaeval witches, especially in Italy, but plenty of evidence exists that she is one and the same with Titania, the 'Fairy Queen.'" Lewis Spence, *British Fairy Origins* (Wellingborough, England: The Aquarian Press, 1946), p. 138.

[5] Theodore Spencer, *Shakespeare and the Nature of Man* (New York: Collier Books, 1966), p. 5.

[6] E. M. W. Tillyard, *The Elizabethan World Picture* (New York: Vintage Books, n.d.), p. 25.

[7] See Sir John Davies's poem, "Orchestra."

[8] Mircea Eliade, *Cosmos and History: The Myth of the Eternal Return* (New York: Harper Torchbooks, 1959), p. 23.

[9] *Ibid.*, p. 25.

[10] Erich Neumann, "On the Moon and Matriarchal Consciousness," *Dynamic Aspects of the Psyche* (New York: The Analytical Psychology Club, 1956), p. 49.

[11] Isaiah, 64:4: "For since the beginning of the world men have not heard, nor perceived by the ear, neither hath the eye seen, O God, beside thee, what he hath prepared for him that waiteth for him."

I Corinthians, 2:9: "But as it is written, Eye hath not seen, nor ear heard, neither have entered into the heart of man, the things which God hath prepared for them that love him."

[12] Rudolph Otto writes of experiences of the divine as "surmises or inklings of a Reality fraught with mystery and momentousness . . . [and] the groping, hesitant, tentative manner in which the meaning of the experience always reveals itself" (*The Idea of the Holy*, New York: Oxford University Press, p. 147).

[13] Nor Hall, *The Moon and the Virgin* (New York: Harper & Row, 1980), p. 59.

[14] This reminds us of Bottom, who also has multiple sides to himself. Early in the play, when he and his friends are rehearsing for *Pyramus and Thisbe*, Bottom has the part of Pyramus but wants to play Hercules, Thisbe, and the lion as well!

[15] Jeffrey Burton Russell, *Witchcraft in the Middle Ages* (Ithaca, NY: Cornell University Press, 1972), p. 52.

[16] Ann Ulanov, *The Feminine* (Evanston, IL: Northwestern University Press, 1971), p. 177.

[17] Madeleine Doran, "Introduction," *Dream*, p. 24.

[18] Herbert Marcuse, One-Dimensional Man (Boston: Beacon Press, 1966), pp. xi, 15, xiii.

[19] In *The Golden Ass*, a second century A.D. prose tale by the Greek writer Apuleus, the protagonist Lucius is completely transformed into an ass and has many adventures in his animal shape. He is restored to human form through the intervention of the goddess Isis. Shakespeare might have known this work in translation.

7

Sir Gawain and
the Green Knight

The Goddess is manifest in the world; she brings life into being,
is nature, *is* flesh. Union is not sought outside the world in some
heavenly sphere or through dissolution of the self into the void
beyond the senses. Spiritual union is found in life, within nature,
passion, sensuality—through being fully human, fully one's self.

—*Starhawk*

*This medieval tale from the Arthurian cycle (ca. 1370) recounts
a series of challenges between a magical immortal Green
Knight, and the very human Sir Gawain. The Green Knight
appears at King Arthur's court and challenges the assembled
company to strike a blow that will sever his head. Only Gawain
accepts the challenge. The terms of the challenge specify that
one year hence, Gawain must present himself to receive a similar blow from the Green Knight at a green chapel in the woods.
Gawain strikes the blow, and the Green Knight picks up his
severed head and leaves the court. On the way to keeping his
part of this fearful bargain, Gawain accepts the hospitality of Sir
Bertilak and his young, beautiful wife for the three days before
he must appear to meet the Green Knight's challenge. Bertilak
offers to exchange whatever game he brings home from his daily
hunt for whatever Gawain accepts from Bertilak's young wife.
The first two days, Gawain exchanges the kisses he has received*

for the game Bertilak has brought home. On the third day,
Gawain exchanges the kisses, but keeps secret a magic green
girdle that the lady has said will keep him from bodily harm.
Gawain goes to his fateful meeting only to discover that the
Green Knight and Bertilak are one and the same. The Green
Knight laughs at Gawain's humanity in wishing to live more
than to be perfectly truthful. Gawain, however, feels great shame
at not being perfect, and vows to wear the green girdle forever
as an outward sign of his failure. When his fellows at court hear
the whole story, they vow to also wear a green baldric, so that
Gawain's shame becomes a badge of honor for them all.

In *A Midsummer Night's Dream* there is a plenitude of metamorphosis, of foolish humanity, love, relatedness, and community between people and between the human world and the divine. It is the realm of the divine feminine. When we turn to *Sir Gawain and the Green Knight*,[1] we enter the realm of the solitary man intent on achieving his own fulfillment. Gawain is not intent on being multiple and connected to others, but is rather single-minded, solitary, and striving to be perfect. There is much to laugh about in *Dream*, and in *Sir Gawain* we hear the laughter of Bertilak and of Arthur's court; but Sir Gawain *cannot* laugh at himself. The young Sir Gawain thus reflects the tragic self-centeredness of our male-dominated culture and its values.

Sir Gawain is a story of a man's obsession with being perfect, a solitary and, ultimately, lonely obsession that grows out of cultural expectations we still struggle with today. In his compulsion to be perfectly moral and perfectly courageous and in his subsequent remorse at discovering that he is less than perfect, Sir Gawain reveals that he is blind to both how moral he is and the remarkable courage he displays. It is as if because he cannot *completely control* who he is according to his plan of perfection for himself, he cannot accept any part of who he is in reality! Gawain is a classic victim of the all-or-nothing ethos of the patriarchal world view. Morgan Le Fay, the great Celtic goddess, functions in this story as a source of the counterbalancing wisdom of the feminine. It is a wisdom of accepting *imperfection*, the body, and one's physical and pluralistic humanity. It takes great courage to accept who you are instead of forever striving to be someone better, someone other than who you are. Ironically, this kind of focus on a better self, a future self that one does not yet inhabit, keeps us from living the present and living in our bodies. It is no wonder that this striving for perfection is so deeply rooted in patriarchy. This striving for perfection is like striving to become a Platonic ideal, a process that necessarily involves rejection and repudiation of the reality of the flesh.

In *Addiction to Perfection,* Marion Woodman points to *Macbeth,* specifically to Lady Macbeth, as emblems of our male-dominated culture's unforgiving and self-destructive nature; she might just as well have chosen this fourteenth-century Arthurian tale with its metaphoric vision. Woodman's thesis, has, for me, a clear connection to Sir Gawain:

> Essentially I am saying that many of us—men and women—are
> addicted in one way or another because our patriarchal culture
> emphasizes specialization and perfection. Driven to do our best at
> school, on the job, in our relationships—in every corner of our
> lives—we try to make ourselves into works of art. Working so hard to
> create our own perfection we forget that we are human beings.[2]

Woodman suggests that the more we are driven by these cultural standards and images of perfection, however they are defined, the less we are able to accept our imperfect bodies and lives. We are driven to look perfect, to have the objects denoting the ideal life, and to arrive at socially determined versions of personal success. Obviously since none of us can either achieve or maintain these criteria as static, unchanging, fixed points, we tend to devalue ourselves accordingly. As Woodman writes: "Indeed, *perfection is defeat* . . . perfection belongs to the gods; completeness or wholeness is the most a human being can hope for."[3]

It is not that we should teach forgiveness, which implies that we should still be striving for perfection, but that we be willing to accept forgiveness for falling short. We need to name and celebrate our imperfectability as what it *means* to be fully human. Being perfect, I think, is the wrong goal to have because it is fixed and unidimensional. Sir Gawain, the fourteenth-century knight, needs to be reminded that human perfection is a contradiction in terms and that he should not think of himself a failure because he fails to be perfect. The inherent value of such great stories is that they show us that being human means always to be contradictory. We are mortal with immortal longings, fallible because of our desire to be perfect, in conflict yet longing to be free of our troubles. This duality *is* our destiny; a destiny we violate by deprecating it with a monistic vision of ourselves.

Herbert Marcuse, in *One-Dimensional Man*, presents us with another highly critical perspective on our repressive culture of technological rationality; it "lead[s] to the triumph of the one-dimensional reality over all contradiction."[4] Marcuse doesn't directly address perfection as a value, but his book is a devastating critique of the ways our culture systematically reduces the possibility of our experiencing the manifold into a single experience. "Multi-dimensional language is made into one-dimensional language, in which different and conflicting meanings no longer interpenetrate but are kept apart; the explosive historical dimension of meaning is silenced."[5]

Literature, and the classics in particular, are a part of this historical dimension of meaning; it is not yet silenced, because it often seeks to explore this conflict. Like Gilgamesh, Macbeth, and Willie Loman, Sir Gawain is so driven by an inner single-mindedness that he is in great danger of completely devaluing the whole of his life. Because of his obsession with achieving the abstractions of perfect, unmitigated morality and courage, he fails to own or live inside his tangible and multiple reality as a flawed (but good and courageous) person. Marion Woodman maintains, "Living by principles is not living your own life. It is easier to try to be better than who you are than to *be* who you are."[6] Ironically, holding perfection as the highest value becomes a way of devaluing all the richness that life, with its myriad flaws and imperfections, can have.

The most striking features about *Sir Gawain* as a story are the awesome terrors of the supernatural and Sir Gawain's steadfastness in courageously facing those terrors. In *Macbeth* and *Dream,* the supernatural events are minor in comparison. *Sir Gawain and the Green Knight* is a story of a man's anticipated rendezvous with his own death, a rendezvous he courageously meets and survives.

The first terror in the story is visually stunning. The Green Knight appears as a giant among men. He is colored completely green with a great beard and hair flowing down to his elbows. He appears as a huge man riding an equally massive green horse. The man and his mount come riding into the court of King Arthur on New Year's Day, as the assembled company is eating and drinking.

> Such a horse, such a horseman, in the whole wide world
> Was never seen or observed by those assembled before,
> Not one. (lls. 197–199)

Symbolic of his duality of life and death, he carries a cluster of holly in one hand and a huge axe in the other. Only later do we learn his allegiance to the goddess Morgan.[7] He is no mortal man, but "a phantom from Fairyland" (l. 240) who leaves all of Arthur's brave knights daunted and suddenly, *appropriately,* silent. Clearly the visitation of the the Green Knight is an experience of the numinous, of awe, of divine paradox.[8] The Green Knight is probably the most famous Green Man in literature—because of his color, his emblems of the holly and the axe, representing life and death, and because of his powers of regeneration and his allegiance to the feminine and the goddess Morgan. Burton Raffel describes him as being "partly human, partly a force of nature."[9] His role in this story is to reveal to Gawain and to us that being human means to be a force of nature, part of a cycle of growth, decay, and regeneration. Paradoxically, he shows us how to be human by showing us how to learn from nature.

As if his appearance at court were not enough, he offers to challenge one of Arthur's knights to what he calls "a Christmas game" (l. 283), proposing an exchange of axe blows spaced a year and a day apart, beginning with the one he is willing to receive now from a challenger at Arthur's court. But there were no challengers from Arthur's court! Arthur's knights sat in stunned silence until Arthur himself stepped forward. Sir Gawain then volunteered, to spare Arthur harm and the shame of having no liege man courageous enough to accept a challenge from this otherworldly giant.

Sir Gawain distinguishes himself by being the only knight of the Round Table with the courage to play in the Green Knight's bizarre and frightening Christmas game. Sir Gawain strikes his blow with the axe and beheads the Green Knight, but the Knight does not die. The Green Knight simply retrieves his head and carries on:

> Holding his head by the hair in his hand.
> He settled himself in the saddle as steadily
> As if nothing had happened to him, though he had
> No head. (ll. 436–439)

And then the head speaks to Gawain:

> Be prepared to perform what you promised . . .
> Go to the Green Chapel . . . to get . . .
> Such a stroke as you have struck. (ll. 448;451;453)

The full impact of the game is now apparent. Sir Gawain and everyone else know that in a year and a day he must receive a similar blow from the immortal Green Knight, a blow Sir Gawain believes he cannot survive. From this moment until he meets the Green Knight a year and a day hence, Sir Gawain is anticipating his death. Gawain's story is about how he confronts and acknowledges his mortality. For all his devotion to the ideal of Christian, knightly perfection, Sir Gawain is human. He has a vulnerable, mortal body that can perish, and his death is now only a year and a day away.

Sir Gawain is about two covenants, which are adroitly intertwined at the end of the story. The first is the Christmas game between Gawain and the Green Knight. The second takes place a year later when Gawain, on his way to meet the Green Knight again, stays for three nights in the castle of Sir Bertilak. In return for Sir Bertilak's hospitality, Gawain agrees to exchange whatever he receives each day for whatever game Bertilak brings back from hunting. On the first two days, Gawain accepts some kisses from Bertilak's young, seductive wife and exchanges them for the game his host has killed. On the third day, he receives three kisses and a green protecting girdle, or baldric, from Bertilak's wife, but he doesn't offer the girdle to Bertilak. Fearful about his meeting with the Green Knight, he keeps the magic girdle a secret from his host because he trusts what Bertilak's wife has said of it:

> For the man that binds his body with this belt of green,
> As long as it is lapped closely about him,
> Is safe from assailants, whoever strives to slay him,
> For he cannot be killed by any cunning there is. (ll. 1851–54)

When Bertilak returns, Gawain gives the kisses to his host. No mention is made of the magic girdle. Concealing the girdle is Gawain's only transgression. In addition to his courage in coming to fulfill the terms of the first contract, Sir Gawain demonstrates great moral restraint as well. Throughout his stay with Sir Bertilak he has resisted the sexual advances of Bertilak's young wife. It is appropriate that he wears the magic girdle that can save his life under his clothes, next to his body. Successful as he is in refusing Lady Bertilak's desire, he is not successful at denying his *own* desire to live. In deciding to keep the girdle, Gawain "pondered, and it appeared to him . . . it would be a splendid stratagem to escape being slain" (ll. 1855;58). His desire to live makes Gawain very human; but, as we discover at the end, it is this very humanness for which Gawain castigates himself.

On the day Sir Gawain leaves Bertilak's castle to meet the Green Knight, the weather has turned wild, with cold "inflicting on the flesh flails from the north" (l. 2002). The day with its body-stinging cold, and the whole year leading up to it, seem to function as occasions for Gawain to more fully accept his mortality and the body's own stratagems for survival. After all, he is en route to a fatal encounter; a lesser man might simply ride off in another direction and claim that he never found the Green Chapel! Overcoming patriarchal notions of abstract perfection is something that takes time, certainly more than a year. The whole of the tale is really about the beginning of Gawain's descent from his sense of his perfection into the depths of his humanity.

Gawain dresses, carefully wrapping the magic "lace belt, the lady's gift," (l. 2030) around himself and sets out with a squire to ride to the Green Chapel. Scholars have suggested that this man who comes along as a guide "is the Green Knight in yet another shape."[10] The Green Knight's changing, flexible self embodies multiplicity, in direct contrast to Sir Gawain's apparent rigidity.[11] The squire tries to frighten Gawain out of facing the Green Knight; and, when this fails, parts company with Gawain, giving him final directions to the Chapel. The directions suggest a descent into the underworld where encounters with the realm of the divine feminine await him:

> Ride down this rough track round yonder cliff
> Till you arrive in a rugged ravine at the bottom,
> Then look about on the flat, on your left hand,
> And you will view there in the vale that very chapel,
> And the grim gallant who guards it always. (ll. 2144–48)

Once he has arrived in this landscape of layered depths, Gawain finds what is called "a fairy mound." It is extensively described:

> A smooth-surfaced barrow by the side of a stream
> Which flowed forth there in a fall of water,
> Foaming and frothing as if feverishly boiling.
> . . .
> It had a hole in each end and on either side,
> And was overgrown with grass in great patches.
> All hollow it was within, only an old cavern
> Or the crevice of an ancient crag: he could not explain it
>   Aright. (ll. 2171; 2172–74; 2180–84)

To anyone familiar with Neolithic chambers, passage graves, and the "fairy mounds" scattered throughout the British Isles, this description strikes a powerful chord. These sites are thought by many who have seen and studied them to have been dedicated to the Goddess.

> Woman-centered culture, based on the worship of the Great Goddess, underlies the beginnings of all civilization. Mother Goddess was carved on the walls of paleolithic caves, and painted in the shrines of the earliest cities, those of the Anatolian plateau. For her were raised the giant stone circles, the henges of the British Isles, the dolmens and cromlechs of the later Celtic countries, and for her the great passage graves of Ireland were dug.[12]

The "old cavern" is reminiscent of Calypso's cave in *The Odyssey* (note the presence of sacred springs, widely held as sacred to the Goddess, near both caves), and the cliffside cave where Jim and Huck ride out the storm in *Huckleberry Finn*.[13] This barrow is also a kind of green chapel that Gawain calls "the most evil holy place I ever entered" (l. 2196). It is certainly a place of paradox, for here a Christian knight is about to receive some much-needed pagan wisdom.

In the climactic scene of the poem, the Green Knight steps forward to return Gawain's blow. Gawain bows, exposing his neck, and stifles his fear. The Green Knight feigns two blows and Gawain flinches at the first. The third and final blow merely nicks Gawain's neck, cutting him so that he bleeds slightly but is otherwise unscathed. The Green Knight reveals that he is, in fact, Lord Bertilak. The two feigned blows were for the two days Gawain honestly and honorably returned the gifts of kisses, and the third tiny nick was for the minor transgression on Gawain's part of keeping the magic baldric. Reflecting the values of the Green Man, Bertilak says:

> here your faith failed you, you flagged somewhat, sir,
> Yet it was not for a well-wrought thing, nor for
>   wooing either,
> But for love of your life, which is less blameworthy.
> (ll. 2366–68)

But this is not how Sir Gawain sees it. Gawain rages against himself and shakes in a torrent of anger:

> [He was] so filled with fury that his flesh trembled,
> And the blood from his breast burst forth in his face.
> He shrank for shame at what the chevalier spoke of.
> (ll. 2396–98)

Gawain then upbraids himself, revealing:

> I being craven about our encounter . . .
> Connived with covetousness to corrupt my nature
> And the liberality and loyalty belonging to chivalry.
> Now I am faulty and false and found fearful always.
> (ll. 2405–8)

The lines reveal alienation, a feeling of self-importance, and an almost predestined finality. Gawain shows how little love he has for himself. He is so bound up in his need to be perfect and his sense of self-control and ownership of himself. He even claims that his action to save himself has corrupted his nature! The nature he had planned for himself did not take his body and his instinct for survival into account. Not only has this instinct to survive, which Bertilak calls "love of your life," overturned his plans for perfection, it also has corrupted "the liberality and loyalty belonging to chivalry." In effect, because Gawain is not perfect, he has brought about a corruption of chivalry itself. What is more, Gawain sees all of this as true forever. Gawain's anguish is genuine, and it parallels what Marion Woodman says of people driven by the ruthlessness of the masculine principle:

> The anguish in the individual is no less than the anguish in the
> culture. Without the sacred rites to contain and help transform our
> fear and guilt, we as individuals tend to fall into aloneness. . . . In
> earlier centuries, the hero (the courageous masculine spirit) exerted

his strength to conquer his overwhelming instinctual drives. He was
ashamed to surrender in war. He was afraid to surrender to loving
arms, for fear of losing himself. Our civilization is the flower of his
courage.[14]

The characterization fits Gawain aptly. He is ashamed to surrender to
his humanity, to his natural bodily instincts, or to accept who he is as
opposed to who he thinks he should be. To surrender for Gawain would
mean to become human, *like the rest of us*. He is invited by Bertilak to
return to his home to meet Morgan Le Fay, a goddess who is also
Gawain's aunt.[15] It was she who designed both covenants: "Therefore I
beg you, bold sir, come back to your aunt, / Make merry in my house,
for my men love you" (ll. 2489–90). When he returns to Arthur's court,
the knights and ladies laugh at Gawain's extreme, excessive guilt. The
knights, remembering *their* fear and cowardice in the presence of the
Green Knight, agree to wear the symbolic green baldric themselves, in
a "sacred rite to contain and help transform [Gawain's] fear and guilt."
But Gawain will not be consoled. He, as Woodman points out, has
fallen into aloneness, an aloneness that ironically has been present all
along in the very value system of perfection, which carries in it a deeply
elitist undercurrent.

Gawain refuses Bertilak's invitation "to revel for the rest of this
rich feast" (l. 2401) at his home with his wife and the older woman,
Morgan, and delivers a speech against women, projecting his misogyny
back to Eve and the way Adam "was . . . taken in" by a woman (l.
2416). Gawain extends the list of great men (like himself) who suc-
cumbed to women's wiles to include Solomon, Samson, and David.
His speech underscores how arrogant, egotistical, and ultimately superior his notion of perfection is. His deep sense of personal failure, his
anger against women, his rejection of his family ties to the Goddess,
and his refusal to accept the warmth and love of the court itself show
how reductive, narrow, cold, and solitary his ideal of perfection has
been all along. By being perfect, Gawain seeks to be set above others,
above family and communal ties, and above his very human nature.
This is the lesson he must now learn. He must see and accept that in
being human and fallible, he is part of the rest of us, and he is part of
nature.

When Sir Gawain rides out to meet his rendezvous with the Green

Knight, he carries a shield with "the Pentangle in pure gold depicted thereon." (l. 643) It is described as a five-pointed star, "and the English call it, / . . . the Endless Knot."[16] It is used here as a symbol of the five wounds of Christ and therefore a symbol of Christian perfection. Gawain rides back to court wearing the green girdle (which Bertilak calls "a *perfect* token . . . of the great adventure at the Green Chapel" (ll. 2398–99; italics mine) not *under* his garments, but "bound by his side / And laced under the left arm with a lasting knot" (ll. 2486–87). He explains it to the court:

> This is the figure of the faithlessness that was found in me,
> Which I must needs wear while I live.
> For sin cannot be concealed without sorry luck succeeding,
> Since, when it is once fixed, it will never be worked loose.
> (ll. 2509–12)

With a symbol of Christian perfection on his shield, Gawain rides forth to a great adventure. His encounter with Lord and Lady Bertilak, the strange barrow in a vale, and the three blows from the Green Knight-as-Bertilak, are all of it designed and instigated by the Celtic goddess figure, Morgan Le Fay. When Gawain returns, no mention is made of the Endless Knot on his shield (a form of armor carried away from *the body*); but he wears the green baldric, his token of imperfection, over his armour tied in "a lasting knot." The green sash with gold lace trim[17] is a beautiful article of clothing, feminine, vulnerable, and human; in its own paradoxical way, it is a kind of armor against the terrible fragmentation and loss of humanity that come from pursuing perfection as the only goal. Would that we all might learn to wear our humanity with such grace and pride! At the end of the tale, the baldric represents a third covenant between Gawain and the Goddess for him to become fully human. It will not be an easy one for him to fulfill.

Personal Commentary

I don't think I fully understood *Sir Gawain* for myself until I read Marion Woodman's book, *Addiction to Perfection*. The connection I've made to the book has more to do with the results of control and manipulation than with any single ethos of perfection. We miss the point of *Sir Gawain* if we see it only in the light of a medieval quest for Christian perfection. Probably few of us today would find the failure to achieve that ideal, or any strict religious goal, as especially poignant in our lives. More to the point, I think, is that many men and women will connect with Gawain's rigid self-control, his wish to keep his whole life under the rule of his mind, and the remorse he feels having lost perfect self-government. I can't really say that I maintain any strict life regimen as Gawain does, but at the same time I cannot say that I am free from remorse that I don't. In other words, if I do not have Gawain's perfection, neither do I have the Green Knight's generous and expansive self-acceptance. It is easier for me to identify with Gawain's sense of pained failure and keep myself in line than it is to identify with and experience the Green Knight's warm, forgiving laughter.

There is an unforgiving drivenness at the heart of *Sir Gawain* that is remarkably modern and is not by any means exclusively male. We are bombarded on all fronts by media images of and stories about people with perfect faces and bodies and lucrative, successful lives; in comparison, the rest of us are nobodies. There is always a faster lane somewhere, full of beautiful men and women who "have it all." Few of us exposed to these images can escape some sense of failure or of not having fully "arrived." We are continually challenged to find and maintain self-acceptance. A self-acceptance that can wear a green baldric of failure and laughs at itself in forgiveness seems an authentic ideal to hold.

---

[1] *Sir Gawain and the Green Knight*, translated by Brian Stone (Baltimore, MD: Penguin Books, 1964). This is the text used throughout and henceforth is referred to as *Sir Gawain*.

[2] Marion Woodman, *Addiction to Perfection* (Toronto: Inner City Books, 1982), p. 10.

[3] *Ibid.*, p. 51.

[4] Herbert Marcuse, *One-Dimensional Man* (Boston: Beacon Press, 1964) p. 124.

[5] *Ibid.*, p. 198.

[6] Woodman, p. 61.

[7] "The Goddess is first of all earth, the dark, nurturing mother who brings forth all life. She is the power of fertility and generation; the womb, and also the receptive tomb, the power of death. All proceeds from Her; all returns to Her." Starhawk, *The Spiral Dance* (San Francisco: Harper & Row, 1979), p. 78.

[8] ". . . the fairy-story proper only comes into being with the element of the 'wonderful,' with miracle and miraculous events and consequences, i.e., by means of

an infusion of the numinous." Rudolf Otto, *The Idea of the Holy* (New York: Oxford University Press, 1980), p. 122.

⁹ Burton Raffel, "Introduction," *Sir Gawain and the Green Knight* (New York: New American Library, 1970), p. 27.

¹⁰ *Sir Gawain*, note, p. 107.

¹¹ When Marion Woodman writes in the Preface to *Addiction to Perfection*, "This book is about a beheading" (p. 7), she means it is about "beheading" the culture's excessive devotion to the abstract masculine goals of perfection. In the light of this comment it is not irrelevant that the Green Knight can *lose* his head and live: he is *more* than just his head; he is his body as well, so his life-force goes on with or without it.

¹² Starhawk, "Witchcraft and Women's Culture," in Womanspirit Rising, eds. Carol Christ and Judith Plaskow (New York: Harper & Row, 1979), p. 260.

¹³ The stage directions for Act IV, scene I of Mac*beth*, the scene in which the Weird Sisters present him with the three apparitions, are usually depicted as "A Cavern."

¹⁴ Woodman, p. 123.

¹⁵ Morgan is Arthur's half-sister, and Arthur is an uncle to Gawain. So Gawain has a goddess figure in his family tree.

¹⁶ *Sir Gawain*, Appendix Six, p. 135.

¹⁷ As an emblem of the many-sided feminine itself, the sash is described variously in the poem as "a glittering girdle" (123), "a baldric" (125), "a band" (125), "that braided belt" (118), "the lace belt, the lady's gift" (105), "the love-lace" (98), "a girdle of green silk with a golden hem" (97).

8

The Death of Ivan Ilyich

Every goddess is larger, fiercer, more dangerous seen through the haze of patriarchal denial and longing. Death denied feeds on fear, grows dense, becomes material in ways that don't allow the light to transfigure the shadows. Paradoxically, Death honored brings clarity and courage . . . like labor, the presence of Death propels one . . . fully into the now.

—*Pam Wright*

Tolstoy's short novel (1886) depicts Ivan Ilyich's relentless pursuit of status in terms of his legal career and his upper-middle-class social standing. While his attention is focused on a superficial ascent in the eyes of others, his body is undergoing a slow descent into death. The reality of this consequence has never figured in Ivan's plans for himself. Moreover, he is largely shunned by his family and friends, who find his slow death very unseemly. Only one person, the peasant Gerasim, comes to Ivan's deathbed and comforts him. In the course of his dying in the company of such a loving, compassionate man, Ivan slowly begins to accept his mortality and realizes how empty of human warmth and depth his life has been.

111

Central to the last three works I've examined are encounters with the numinous, experiences that are "wholly other."[1] The three Weird Sisters in *Macbeth*, Titania in *A Midsummer Night's Dream* and the Green Knight in *Sir Gawain and the Green Knight* present us with what C.S. Lewis calls *Longaevi* (literally "longlivers"). He prefers this word to "fairies" because:

> That word, tarnished by pantomime and bad children's books with worse illustrations . . . might encourage us to bring to the subject some ready-made, modern concept of a Fairy and to read the old texts in the light of it. Naturally, the proper method is the reverse; we must go to the texts with an open mind and learn from them what the word *fairy* meant to our ancestors.[2]

Lewis describes what that word meant to our ancestors as bringing "a welcome hint of wildness and uncertainty into a universe that is in danger of being a little too self-explanatory, too luminous . . ." as "all affect[ing] the mind in the same way [with a] vision which startles by its otherness."[3] In spite of every effort to discern or classify the nature of these creatures, "to find a socket into which the Fairies would fit," they are, finally, "marginal, fugitive creatures. . . . No agreement was achieved. As long as the Fairies remained at all they remained evasive."[4]

Of course, the reason they would fit no "socket" is that they were not a tool or appliance of the self-explanatory, luminous, patriarchal universe. Fairies are about changes in consciousness, about visions that startle because they are embodiments of the matriarchal universe. Fairies are what Banquo calls "instruments of darkness telling us truths." They are experiential forms of a consciousness that has been systematically expunged from the patriarchal view of reality. Naturally, they would seem startling and "other"—at least until driven away totally through trivialization and dismissal as superstition.

I contend that Fairies are forms of the numinous, experiences of otherness, because patriarchal consciousness, with its emphasis on what Lewis calls "sockets" and Herbert Marcuse calls "technological rationality,"[5] has made them so. What is more, this dominant, reductive consciousness has dismissed them totally. The Weird Sisters come into Macbeth's ken to restore balance in his consciousness, to broaden his "single state of man" (what Marcuse would call his "one-dimensionality"). They come to open Macbeth to other possibilities, other ways of thinking and being. Oberon, Titania, Puck, and the Fairies in *Dream* are there to restore the balance of consciousness in Theseus' Athens, to bring magic and change and multiplicity into a kingdom of one-dimensionality. In *Sir Gawain and the Green Knight,* that "phantom from fairyland" in the person of the Green Knight or Bertilak, tries, using fear, trembling, and Fairy subterfuge, what Lewis calls "mingled ferocity and geniality,"[6] to shake Sir Gawain out of his obsession with perfection so he might experience a balanced humanity that Bertilak calls "love of your life."

In *One-Dimensional Man* Marcuse points out, "Epistemology is in itself ethics, and ethics is epistemology."[7] That is, if consciousness allows only *one way* of knowing the world, it will allow only *one way* of behaving in the world. If we, like Theseus in *Dream,* dismiss what poets, lovers, and madmen *know;*we can only behave or carry out the ethics implicit in our one-dimensional way of knowing the world. What a paradox! If we, like Sir Gawain, become locked into a notion of human perfection that excludes the vision of humanity, we have become exceedingly imbalanced. *The Death of Ivan Ilyich* presents us with a striking example of the rigidity of this kind of epistemology and ethics in practice.

Ivan Ilyich is really a kind of modern Sir Gawain, differing only in the way he defines perfection. Ivan Ilyich is a man completely devoted to having a perfect bourgeois, conformist life or, as we might say today, lifestyle. Ilyich is a member of the Russian middle-class of the 1880s who would be completely at home in middle-class America of the late twentieth century. Ivan Ilyich may wish to be thought of as *upper* middle class, but then that is part of his problem and ours.

He is a character so deeply entrenched in his quest to acquire the perfect life that what passes for social propriety is all that matters to him. It is all he knows, and it governs all his actions. He is a man immured in the reductive world of conformity, duty, and respectability; he is impervious to the numinous in all its forms except one, his own death. In his world, which no longer entertains the possibilities of numinous experience, there are no chinks in the armor of the patriarchal, one-dimensional consciousness to permit the intrusion of "a welcome hint of wildness and uncertainty."[8] Therefore the experience of the numinous must come not from without, but from within. It appears in the form of Ivan's death, which he tries to deny, and looms ever larger until it engulfs him.

The preposterous reach of Tolstoy's novel is a great gift. It addresses the paradoxical essence of life: that life and death are like lovers, woven together in the greatest, most sacred *hierosgamos* of all. The story is about how to live and how to die, *not* as two separate issues, but as two sides of the same question. The rules for living in a death-denying culture don't include how to die because death breaks all the rules. It undoes our perfection and makes a disorderly mess of our lives. At the heart of our patriarchal culture is the longing to control *everything*—to master even death and keep it at bay. In *The Death of Ivan Ilyich*, Tolstoy reminds us that this is a lie that will give death the ultimate ironic mastery when it comes because we have tried to ignore it so long. The only right relationship we can have with death is not domination but coexistence, by knowing, owning, and living inside Death's shadow as a part of our lives. When we confront death in the way we *live*, we bear it close to us (where it always is, anyway) and it makes life sufficient. Tolstoy suggests in this book that the answer to the question, "How should I live?" is: "By not denying *your* death or the deaths of others."

There are many painful and terrible moments in *Ivan Ilyich*. For me, one of the most telling is early on in the novel when we learn, quite matter-of-factly, that two of Ivan's children have died:

> They moved, they were short of money, and his wife disliked the new town. Although his salary was higher, the cost of living was greater; moreover, two of their children had died, and so family life became even more unpleasant for Ivan Ilyich. (pp. 58–59)

The children are not named, their ages are not given, and no cause of death is ever mentioned. Clearly there was no memorable grief for Ivan or his wife, only more unpleasantness. Tolstoy writes: "Ivan Ilyich's life had been most simple and commonplace—and most horrifying" (p. 49). This is why the only experience powerful enough to cause him to feel any depth, or compassion, is the slow, steady, inexorable, and painful approach of his own death.

Ivan is a man absorbed in his own advancement up the ladder of success in the judicial system: "His entire interest in life was centered in the world of official duties. . . . He went on living this way for another seven years. His daughter was then sixteen years old; another child had died; and one son remained, a school boy, the subject of dissension." (pp. 59, 60) The dissension centers on where to send his son to school. There is only a passing mention of the child who died, and no mention at all of any emotional response to it on the part of either Ivan *or* his wife. They seem reduced by the materialism and superficiality of their culture to functioning mechanically within the system. Ivan's response to his children's deaths as "unpleasantness" will return to haunt him when it is his turn to die:

> He saw that the awesome, terrifying act of his dying had been degraded by those about him to the level of a chance unpleasantness, a bit of unseemly behavior (they reacted to him as they would to a man who emitted a foul odor on entering a drawing room); that it had been degraded by that very "propriety" to which he had devoted his entire life. (p. 103)

Ivan devotes his life completely to vanity, the veneer of fashion, and pleasantness. As he dies slowly from within, his outer life turns unfashionably odious and ugly.

The Goddess is often associated with the Great Round of Nature, with life and death, with seeds that are planted, blossom, and are harvested—and by extension, therefore, with accountability.[9] The way we live our lives is like a seed that grows, bears fruit, and has consequences for which we are answerable. The way Ivan Ilyich dies is emblematic of his accountability for how he has lived.

Tolstoy uses terms like "propriety," "*comme il faut,*" "the rules," etc., almost to the point of excess to drive home for all of us the terrors inherent in the way things are done within the rules of the patriarchy that governs Ivan's world and our own.[10] Ivan lives his life according to a male-dominated, individualistic, success-oriented, unfeeling patriarchal world view. Tolstoy doesn't let his readers off the hook, for he knows well that they are probably more like Ivan Ilyich than not.

The operating metaphor in patriarchal culture is ascent. We aspire to go up the ladder of success, to go up to heaven. The word aspire itself means "to have great ambition" or, in an older usage, "to rise upward;

soar."[11] In a one-dimensional culture focused on hierarchy, it is the only way to go. A major turning point in the book occurs when Ivan injures his side in a fall from a stepladder (it will be his mortal wound) while engaged in home improvement—hanging curtains. This fall is an important opportunity for him to come to grips with the qualities patriarchy doesn't value, the humble, buried wisdom of compassion. Discussions of tragedy seldom address tragic flaws as failure to achieve expectations within a success-driven culture. Viewed this way, such tragic flaws are not so much personal failings as flaws of a culture that fails to value being close to the rich transcendent possibilities offered within our earthly selves, our mortality. Rosemary Ruether writes of "the revolution of the feminine" bringing about "a world where people are reconciled to their own finitude, where the last enemy, death, is conquered, not by a flight into eternity, but, in that spirit of St. Francis that greets 'Brother Death' as a friend, that completes the proper cycle of the human soul."[12] Merlin Stone addresses patriarchy's fear of earth, darkness, death, and woman when she writes of "the white male":

> He attempts to enslave and control the earth itself. He talks of
> darkness and women and nature as chaotic, in need of his supposedly
> singular ability to create order, but it is his own mortality over which
> he wants to gain control. . . . He is simply, but desperately, trying to
> gain control of death. . . . Perhaps if and when he could accept death
> as a natural part of the life cycle, and not as punishment or sin, his
> fears would dissipate. Perhaps his frantic need to gain control over
> darkness, thus to gain control over his inner image of his own death,
> would disappear. Perhaps someday he would even be able to realize
> that it is actually from the darkness that is earth, from the darkness
> that is woman, that life comes forth. Right now, he talks a lot about
> being filled with light, and enlightenment. I think it is time for us to
> start talking about being filled with the dark, and endarkenment.[13]

The Death of Ivan Ilyich is about this very process of "endarkenment." Ivan comes to see that death is a part of being alive. To be alive is to be married to death in a lifelong *hierosgamos*. The reality of this sacred marriage, this essence deeply affronts Ivan when he first learns he is dying: ". . . it simply was not possible that he should have to die. That would be too terrible. So his feelings went" (p. 94). After Ivan dies, Pyotr Ivanovich, one of his colleagues, has a similar thought and muses that "death was a chance experience that could happen only to Ivan

Ilyich, never to himself" (p. 44). Ivan denies the growing, persistent pain and its import when he refers to the wound as an "It:" ". . . his judicial work could not rescue him from *It*. And the worst thing was that *It* drew his attention not so that he would do anything, but merely so that he would look at *It*, look *It* straight in the face and, doing nothing, suffer unspeakable agony" (p. 95).

This impersonal wound in Ivan's body is referred to as an "It" twenty-one times in the sixth chapter, and slowly becomes personified as Ivan discovers that he cannot ignore its presence. By chapter Nine, Ivan stops avoiding the wound and begins addressing it as "Thou"[14]:

> Why hast Thou done all this? Why hast Thou brought me to this? Why dost Thou torture me so? For what? . . . The pain started up again, but he did not stir, did not call out. He said to himself: 'Go on then! Hit me again! But what for? What for ? What have I done to Thee?' (p. 118)

What he has done is to be utterly *oblivious* to his own pain and the pain of other people's lives. Pain is a dark side of human reality that Ivan has totally shunned; now great physical pain has become a part of his life. I think of Ivan's wound as a sacred wound because it teaches him a way of being in the world that he has systematically erased from his life. In Chapter Four, Ivan has an inkling of all this: "There was no deceiving himself: something new and dreadful was happening to him, something of such *vast importance that nothing in his life could compare with it*" (p. 80; italics mine). Just what that importance is Ivan can't fathom until the moment of death, when his sacred wound brings about the birth of compassion and heart as he takes his final breaths. In his last days, Ivan makes *his* descent to the Goddess; he describes it as "being thrust into a narrow black sack—a deep one" (p. 117), and a descent into "the depths of the sea or the bowels of the earth" (p. 122). Ivan descends into a region that is unimaginable within the boundaries of his dutiful life and the way it ". . . conformed to all the laws, rules, and proprieties" (pp. 123-24). Kathryn Allen Rabuzzi writes that this revelation reflects the "interconnected reversibility of birth and death symbolized by spiral and labyrinth. . . . As in a lengthy birth, Ivan Ilyich's full entry into the sack does not take place immediately. He must first endure an ordeal of self-questioning and physical pain which eventuates in a mystical experience. . . ."[15]

Ivan slowly becomes aware that all his efforts to lead the right life have been "*not the real thing*" (p. 126), and his isolation from colleagues, friends, wife, and children becomes acute. The one person who saves Ivan from complete and utter isolation is Gerasim, a peasant pantry boy who is not afraid to touch Ivan and keeps watch over him all night. With his natural earthiness and vitality, Gerasim brings the healing spirit of the Green Man into Ivan's consciousness; he becomes, metaphorically, 'midwife' to the birth-in-death of Ivan's soul:

> What had induced his moral agony was that during the night, as he gazed at Gerasim's broad-boned, sleepy, good-natured face, he suddenly asked himself: 'What if my entire life, my entire conscious life, simply was *not the real thing*?' It occurred to him that what had seemed utterly inconceivable before—that he had not lived the kind of life he should have—might in fact be true. (p. 126)

Gerasim attends Ivan as he lies dying; he is the only person who does so. He bathes Ivan, takes out the chamber pot, talks with him, and cares for him.

> Gerasim was the only one who understood and pitied him. And for that reason Ivan Ilyich felt comfortable only with Gerasim. It was a comfort to him when Gerasim sat with him sometimes the whole night through holding his legs, refusing to go to bed. . . . (pp. 103-4)

Through his compassion, Gerasim, the lowest person in the social hierarchy, shows that morally and spiritually he is the highest. He teaches Ivan what compassion *is*. Gerasim's teachings are not theoretical or abstract; they come through his *laying hands* on Ivan, his night-long vigils, and his doing the dirty work of Ivan's bath and chamber pot. Tolstoy uses a remarkable birthing image to describe Gerasim's care of Ivan: "Ivan would send for Gerasim from time to time and have him hold his feet on his shoulders. . . . Ivan Ilyich felt better while Gerasim raised his legs" (p. 102). Gerasim holds Ivan in this birthing position, with loving physical contact, and acts as a spiritual midwife to the birth-in-death of Ivan's soul.

At the end, Ivan discovers that "the real thing" is compassion, touching, and grieving for others. When Ivan makes his last descent, "he plunged into the hole and there at the bottom, something was shining" (p. 132). That something is the compassionate soul born of his suffering.

During Ivan's last moments, his son entered the room, grasped his father's hand, and "pressed it to his lips, and began to cry. At that very moment Ivan Ilyich fell through and saw a light, and it was revealed to him that his life had not been what it should have . . . ." (p. 132). Ivan grieves for his son and for his wife. He feels compassion for them during the long ordeal of his dying. "He felt sorry for them, he had to do something to keep from hurting them. To deliver them and himself from this suffering" (p. 133), Ivan finally lets go of his fear of death and accepts it: "Where was death? What death? There was no fear because there was no death. Instead of death there was light. 'So that's it!' he exclaimed. 'What bliss!'" (p. 133). In the act of fully accepting and embracing his own death in its reality and as an act of compassion for his family, Ivan is also embracing paradox. He becomes "filled with the dark, and endarkenment."[16] It is a profoundly illuminating darkness.

Personal Commentary

In *The Death of Ivan Ilyich,* cancer makes Ivan's perfect life and the lives of everyone around him suddenly very imperfect. What is haunting about this story is the potential of such a real threat to our own visions of perfection and order and our linear, settled routines. No one can really prepare for such a catastrophic event. We can only examine our lives and remember to include the possibility of illness, death, loss, and suffering. To me, *The Death of Ivan Ilyich* is about the importance of maintaining some kind of *consciousness* of death as a part of life and a cause for celebration of each moment.

When I was sixteen, my best friend was killed in a car accident. What I remember was the utter chaos his death created in me and my world. It seemed as if there had been an earthquake and the universe had shifted. The sun, the moon, the trees, the clocks, language—everything seemed unreal, askew, and somehow displaced forever. This is the real power of death; and it is all the more powerful when we are not conscious of it. At sixteen, one can be forgiven for having no such consciousness; but Ivan is an adult. He has lost several of his children but refuses the truth and the reality of death. He cannot acknowledge the simple reality of *mememto mori,* the Latin phrase meaning "remember you must die."

Memento mori is not a formula for morbidity. It is about always making our mortality part of our life plan. My daughter tells me the way people live with the threat of earthquakes in California is to make a precise plan of what to do if one strikes. This is simply another kind of healthy, life-affirming *memento mori*. Ivan never takes this into account: "Everything you lived by and still live by is a lie, a deception that blinds you from the reality of life and death" (p. 128). He is a man who builds a life like a house of glass. If the deaths of his children are earthquakes, then he builds his house on the fault line. When the tremors start and the first hairline fractures began to appear, he is incredulous. He lives without a plan to help him survive and learn from his vulnerability. This novel, like death itself, calls us to live close to the ground and remember that it will one day be our home as well.

[1] Rudolf Otto, *The Idea of the Holy* (New York: Oxford University Press, 1980), p. 70.

[2] C.S. Lewis, *The Discarded Image: An Introduction to Medieval and Renaissance Literature* (Cambridge, MA: Cambridge University Press, 1964), p. 122.

[3] *Ibid.*, pp. 122; 126; 129.

[4] *Ibid.*, pp. 138; 122; 138.

[5] Herbert Marcuse, *One-Dimensional Man* (Boston: Beacon Press, 1970), p. xvi.

[6] Lewis, p. 133.

[7] Marcuse, p. 125.

[8] Lewis, p. 122.

[9] See Erich Neumann, *The Great Mother* (Princeton, NJ: Princeton University Press, 1974), pp. 211-39, and Sylvia Perera, *Descent to the Goddess* (Toronto: Inner City Books, 1981), pp. 21-22; 54-55.

[10] Words like "propriety," "duty," "rules," "*comme il faut*," "correct life" and their variations appear in the novel close to thirty times. The text used throughout is *The Death of Ivan Ilyich* by Leo Tolstoy. Translated by Lynn Solotaroff (New York: Bantam Books, 1987).

[11] *American Heritage Dictionary*, William Morris, ed. (Boston: Houghton Mifflin, 1969).

[12] Rosemary Reuther, "Motherearth and the Megamachine: A Theology of Liberation in a Feminine, Somatic and Ecological Perspective," *Womanspirit Rising*, ed. Carol Christ and Judith Plaskow (New York: Harper & Row, 1979), p. 52.

[13] Merlin Stone, "Endings and Origins," *Woman of Power*, Winter 1988 (8), pp. 28, 29.

[14] This is in keeping with Martin Buber's dialogic I-Thou construct for relating to reality.

[15] Kathryn Allen Rabuzzi, *Motherself: A Mythic Analysis of Motherhood*, (Bloomington: Indiana University Press, 1988), p. 206.

[16] Stone, p. 29.

9

The Bear

Vitally, the human race is dying. It is like a great uprooted tree,
with its roots in the air. We must plant ourselves again in the
universe.

—*D. H. Lawrence*

In Faulkner's The Bear *(1942) Ike McCaslin grows from boyhood into manhood shaped by the teaching of Sam Fathers. Sam,
who is half Chickasaw Indian and half Negro, functions as Ike's
spiritual father throughout the book. He teaches Ike how to hunt,
orient himself, and just be in the woods. Ike learns how the
woods and Old Ben (the bear they hunt every year) can be the
greatest teachers of all. As a young man of twenty-one, Ike
discovers some old ledgers in his family store. The ledgers
reveal the racist villainy of his slaveowner grandfather,
Carothers McCaslin. What Ike has learned from Sam Fathers,
his experiences in the woods, and the bear prepares him to
renounce completely the heritage of his father and grandfather,
including his title of ownership to the land, animals, and people.*

Robert Penn Warren has written that "Faulkner's work contains a savage attack on modernity. . . . The modern world is in moral confusion. . . . It is a world in which self-interest, workableness, success, provide the standards. It is a world which is the victim of abstraction and of mechanism. . . ."[1] What we see in *The Bear* is a portrait of the modern world colored by patriarchal consciousness, a male-dominated world view that rejects the wisdom inherent in the archetypes of both the Goddess and the Green Man. Faulkner advances the wisdom of being "concordant . . . with the wilderness" (p. 110), the wisdom involved in having the humility and courage to be in a concordant relationship with the sacred feminine. In *The Bear,* the wilderness and Old Ben embody the sacred feminine in nature. The bear is an "alma mater" (p. 20), an "apotheosis of the old wild life" (p. 7). The bear and the wilderness are the same force, both representing "the deathless and immemorial phases of the mother" (p. 108). Faulkner's novel is about our ever-increasing repudiation of this divine feminine force and how this repudiation poisons our relationships with each other. We have failed, says Faulkner, "to hold the earth mutual and intact in the communal anonymity of brotherhood" (p. 56). In failing Gaia, we fail her family tree as well because it includes all of us. As Norman O. Brown writes in his introduction to Hesiod's *Theogony,* "not only the line of rulers, but, in fact, the whole realm of being is descended from Earth. . . . Earth [is] the great Mother of all."[2]

In Faulkner's *The Bear,* there are two Green Men—Sam Fathers and Ike McCaslin. This short novel focuses primarily on Ike McCaslin's spiritual education and evolution from boyhood to manhood.[3] The force that gives form to that particular evolution is the knowledge of nature and the wilderness he receives from Sam Fathers, the son of a Negro slave and a Chickasaw chief. Moreover, Old Ben, the mythic bear of the story's title, is at the center of both the wilderness and Ike's spiritual education.

> If Sam Fathers had been his mentor and the backyard rabbits and
> squirrels his kindergarten, then the wilderness the old bear ran was his
> college and the old male bear itself, so long unwifed and childless as to
> have become its own ungendered progenitor, was his alma mater. (p. 20)

Alma mater means 'nourishing mother' and was an epithet applied by the Romans to Ceres, goddess of growing vegetation, and Cybele, a nature goddess, as well as other bounteous goddesses.[4] Faulkner makes the bear a paradox of male and female qualities. The bear is androgynous in a mythic way; it is both "the man" (p. 11) and, like the parthenogenic earth goddess Gaia, "its own ungendered progenitor." Because the bear is of such mythic, sacred proportions, everything in the story takes on a resonating sacrality in relation to it, especially Ike's initiation after he learns the spiritual qualities he must have to hunt the bear from Sam Fathers. "To [Ike] they were going not to hunt bear and deer but to keep yearly rendezvous with the bear which they did not even intend to kill. Two weeks later they would return, with *no trophy, no skin*" (p. 8; italics mine). The point here is not the thing, Old Ben the bear, but the encounter with his sacredness.

In the novel, Ike's father, Uncle Buck, has died long ago, and we know nothing of Ike's mother. He finds a spiritual father in Sam, who helps him make a deep intimate and spiritual connection with the wilderness and the feminine in nature:

> He entered his novitiate to the true wilderness with Sam beside him as he had begun his apprenticeship in miniature to manhood after the rabbits and such with Sam beside him, the two of them wrapped in the damp, warm, negro-rank quilt while the wilderness closed behind his entrance as it had opened momentarily to accept him. . . . It seemed to him that at the age of ten he was witnessing his own birth. (p. 9)

Ike is lucky to experience this spiritual birth so early in life and to have a father figure like Sam to act as midwife to it.

The paradox inherent in Sam's teachings reveals a deep, natural wisdom; he tells Ike, "Be scared. You can't help that. But don't be afraid" (p. 18). Sam teaches Ike to know his relationship to the whole, to be humble,[5] have pride, and not be a coward. Faulkner tells us that Sam has this paradoxical combination of virtues when he describes Sam as "an old man, son of a Negro slave and an Indian king, inheritor on the one hand of the long chronicle of a people who had learned *humility* through suffering and learned *pride* through the endurance which survived the suffering . . ." (p. 85; italics mine). In the same extended sentence, Ike is described as "a boy who wished to learn humility and pride in order to become skillful and worthy in the woods, but found himself becoming so skillful so fast that he feared he would never become worthy because he had not learned humility and pride though he had tried" (p. 85).

There are passages like this throughout *The Bear* that strongly suggest that the novel is more about soul-making than it is about hunting. In this sense, *The Bear* is about learning depth and wisdom. It is about being given a sign—becoming worthy enough just to see and encounter Old Ben. For Sam and Ike hunting is a vehicle for a "rendezvous" (p. 8) with a way of being in a deep, sacred relationship with nature. It is in this sense that *The Bear* embodies one of the most highly detailed and exalted encounters with the mythos of the man of nature, the Green Man.

In the course of learning to hunt, learning to become increasingly at one *with* nature, Ike is taught by Sam that if he is ever to encounter the great bear, he must relinquish his defenses, starting with his gun. This is not hunting as most men are taught and know it, but the paradox befits a man of nature who lives from and with, not superior to nature. Ike goes on to discover that giving up his gun is not enough; he must give up all his mechanical, technological defenses against the numinous:

> He had already relinquished, of his will, because of his need, in
> humility and peace and without regret, yet apparently that had not
> been enough, the leaving of the gun was not enough. He stood for a
> moment—a child, alien and lost in the green and soaring gloom of the
> markless wilderness. Then he relinquished completely to it. It was the
> watch and the compass. He was still tainted. He removed the linked
> chain of the one and the looped thong of the other from his overalls
> and hung them on a bush and leaned the stick beside them and
> entered it. (p. 18)

Ike's relinquishments are forms of spiritual, moral, and physical surrender. He gives himself over to nature and enters the wilderness more like a fellow creature of nature than a hunter. He becomes a kind of Green Man, which is what we all once were and have forgotten as we became more civilized. Once Ike leaves behind the artificial, mechanistic symbols of his separation, he has a numinous encounter with Old Ben:

> Then he saw the bear. It did not emerge, appear: it was just there,
> immobile, fixed in the green and windless noon's hot dappling, not as
> big as he had dreamed it but as big as he had expected, bigger,
> dimensionless against the dappled obscurity, looking at him. (p. 19)

The bear may have been present all along, "it was just there," but Ike couldn't see it until he was untainted by his gun, watch, and compass. He has become both *humble,* i.e., reduced to a fellow creature, and *proud,* courageous enough to be able to enter the woods in a vulnerable, open manner.[6]

In teaching Ike about hunting, Sam Fathers, whom Francis Lee Utley calls "the priest,"[7] is really awakening Ike to his own soul, revealing to Ike some of what it is and how to live by it. It is *not* bound up in technological accoutrements. Ike's reward for what he has learned is his encounter with the bear. For a long moment Ike sees the bear "looking at him. Then it moved. It crossed the glade without haste, walking for an instant into the sun's full glare and out of it, and stopped again and looked back at him across one shoulder. Then it was gone" (p. 19).

Martin Buber writes, "The primary word *I-Thou* establishes the world of relation," and says of our life with nature "There the relation sways in gloom, beneath the level of speech. Creatures live and move over against us, but cannot come to us, and when we address them as *Thou,* our words cling to the threshold of speech."[8] Ike has relinquished all the outward signs of his separation from nature, making a wordless "I-Thou" encounter with Old Ben the bear possible. At that moment, Ike and the bear experience each other on equal terms simply as two beings, two fellow *creatures.* For Ike, it is a sign, an encounter with the numinous.

In a philosophical monograph about nature, novelist John Fowles speaks of the Green Man as "the individual experiencer, the 'green man' hidden in the leaves of his or her unique and once-only being."[9] Fowles's concept of relating to nature is remarkably similar to Buber's:

> There is something in the nature of nature, in its presentness, its
> seeming transience, its creative ferment and hidden potential, that
> corresponds very closely with the wild, or green man, in our psyches;
> and it is a something that disappears as soon as it is relegated to
> . . . a status of merely classifiable *thing.* [Nature] waits to be seen
> otherwise, in its individual presentness, and from our individual
> presentness.[10]

In Buber's terms, this something is lost when we turn nature into an "It." Buber writes that in the I-Thou relation to nature our words "cling to the threshold of speech." Fowles says:

so I sit in the namelessness . . . of the Tree. . . It, this namelessness,
is beyond our science and our arts because its secret is being, not
saying . . . [and] this being can be apprehended only by other present
being, only by the living senses and consciousness. . . . Nature's
consolation, its message [is that] it can be known and entered only
by each, and in its now; not by you through me . . . only by you
through yourself or me through myself. We still have this to learn: the
inalienable *otherness* of each, human and *non-human*. . . .[11]

Faulkner's *The Bear,* Buber's *I and Thou,* and Fowles' *The Tree* offer
profound teaching about how to be in a sacred relationship with nature
and other people. In my mind, all three books present the archetypal
figure of the Green Man within as the essence of entering deeply and fully
into right relationship not only with nature, but with other human beings
as well. When we experience a tree or a bear as a sacred presence, it is
sacred because we are experiencing both ourselves and their living otherness as fellow creatures. We become linked by common mortality, finite-
ness, and *creaturehood;* this same awareness is equally appropriate and
important in our relationships with our fellow human beings.

Mythologically, as descendants from Gaia, Mother Earth, or the
Great Goddess, all living beings are members of the same family tree
and share the same blood line. How much closer, how much more like
family, then, are we to other human beings, who share our very blood.
What makes *The Bear* such a profoundly important book for me is that
Faulkner takes all the teachings Ike receives from Sam Fathers and
shows us how Ike applies them in his social and ethical relationships
with other people. They are people whom Ike discovers *are* blood
relatives because of his grandfather "Carothers' doomed and fatal blood
which in the male derivation seemed to destroy all it touched" (p. 83).

In Part IV of the novel Ike, now twenty-one, learns from some old
ledgers in his family's store that his slaveowner grandfather Carothers
McCaslin had raped a slave woman named Eunice, who bore a daughter, Tomasina. Years later, he also rapes Tomasina. When Eunice learns
that Tomasina's pregnancy is the result of this incestuous rape, she
commits suicide. "Such a combination of incest and miscegenation[12]
represents for Ike an image of the evil condition of the South—and of
humanity in general from the beginning of time. Ike determines not to
compromise with this condition."[13]

What Ike does is to continue the process of relinquishing that Sam taught him. Only now he doesn't relinquish his gun, his watch, and his compass; he relinquishes his patrimony, his "father's will" (p. 65). Ike gives up his title of ownership to the land, people, and animals inherited from his grandfather. He relinquishes his connection with "that whole edifice intricate and complex and founded upon injustice and erected by ruthless rapacity and carried on even yet with at times downright savagery not only to the human beings but the valuable animals too . . ." (p. 87).

The spiritual inheritance Ike has received from Sam, his true father, helps him reject the patrimony of his grandfather and father. When Ike realizes that his family's blood is widely shared among the blacks, known and unknown, descended from his grandfather's "ruthless rapacity . . . [and] savagery," his genealogical connection with a wide range of humanity becomes far more than a metaphor. What proliferating ironies there are here: in a racist culture Ike learns about his soul from a man who is part black and part Chickasaw and puts what he learns to use by relinquishing his patrimony of racism because of what he discovers in his Grandfather's ledgers.

This story contains two descents into the underworld. The first is when Ike leaves his tools behind and descends into the heart of the wilderness to encounter Old Ben. The second grows out of the first when Ike learns of his grandfather's villainy and descends into his own heart to give up *all* claims of his inheritance. These two descents are closely related; both require the leaving behind the values of the patriarchy, its technology, and its proprietal assumptions. Ike is able to let go of the family's claim to the land, animals, and people because he learned long ago, witnessing his own birth to the feminine wisdom of the wilderness beside Sam Fathers, that we are not meant to own the land or other creatures, but rather to live "to hold the earth mutual and intact in the communal anonymity of brotherhood" (p. 56). What Ike learns fitting for a member of the family tree of Gaia or Mother Earth, who recognizes his oneness with "the heritage of all, out of the earth, beyond the earth yet of the earth because his too was of the earth's long chronicle, his too because each must share with another in order to come into it and in the sharing they become one for that while, one: for that little while at least one: indivisible . . . ." (p. 97).

Personal Commentary

Our narrow, static patriarchal world view teaches us that our biological parents are parents enough. We live our whole lives denying our need, in times of illness, crisis, and change, for more fathering and mothering from our parents, loved ones, friends, and even our children. What moves me most about *The Bear* is its dynamic and ultimately matriarchal world view of family, fathering, and mothering:

> summer, and fall, and snow, and wet and saprife spring in their ordered
> immortal sequence, the deathless and immemorial phases of the mother
> who had shaped him if any had toward the man he almost was, mother
> and father both to the old man born of a Negro slave and a Chickasaw
> chief who had been his spirit's father if any had, whom he had revered
> and harkened to and loved and lost and grieved. (p. 108)

For me the key phrase is "toward the man he almost was." Ike's manhood is not something defined and static, fixed in time at some arbitrary cut-off point, but changing, overlapping, and evolving. Ike's manhood is as fluid as Faulkner's prose. Aren't we all, in reality, always moving *toward* the men and women we *almost* are? Viewed this way, parenting itself becomes a large and lifelong process we do for each other. At different points in our lives, we will all be like children in need of fathering and mothering, or else will be called upon to be mother and father for others.

This was first brought home to me when I was sixteen on a visit to my grandmother in Tulsa, Oklahoma. I had traveled there from Texas with my father, who was, for me, a man of venerable and unwavering authority. When I was alone with my grandmother, I spoke to her about my idea of one day possibly becoming a teacher. She approved of this and later, in the presence of my father, turned my ideas for my future into a kind of parental command from her to my father. She was a tiny, frail woman, but I remember her speaking firmly to my father words such as these: "Now Ken, I want you to see to it that this boy can become a teacher if he wants to." And my father, who was like a god to me, instantly became a mere son to his mother, his parent, and answered softly, almost sheepishly: "Yes, Mother." He was already helping me, encouraging me to become that teacher; but the moment of fluid parental identities was stunning to me. A boy's wishes had become parental

10

To the Lighth

Inferiority feelings, the power drive, anxie
envy, jealousy, and the compulsion to subdue
mainsprings of the patriarchal ego.

—E

Virginia Woolf's To the Lighthouse *(1929)*
thoughts and feelings woven around a few :
concerns the Ramsays, an English family, a
spend a summer holiday together on the Isl
Scottish coast. Very little action happens in
Woolf is much more concerned with what h
and feel and how they relate to one another
the first part of the novel to make an outing
lighthouse. Guests take walks; one particul
is an artist. In the second part of the novel,
of her children have died. In part three, the
of the Ramsay family gather again on the I.
Ramsay, his son James, and daughter Cam
journey to the lighthouse. Throughout the i
portrayed as an almost mythic figure who i
Goddess, while Mr. Ramsay is revealed to
very little knowledge of his inner self. His f
from his lack of inner knowledge.

instructions to a powerful father (now suddenly also a boy) from *his* diminutive mother. The parenting I needed during this part of my life came from many sources as I became the teacher I wanted to be. I drew upon many different people as fathers and mothers for my guidance and upbringing. I continue to do so.

One irony about parenting in *The Bear* that I became aware of while writing this book is that in the course of being "shaped . . . toward the man he almost was," Ike must relinquish a major portion of his male heritage from his father and grandfather. In order to become the man Sam Fathers helped give birth to in the feminine wilderness, Ike will eventually have to repudiate a major portion of the cultural patrimony he learns from the family ledgers. Sometimes sons must *un-father* parts of themselves to become the men they were meant to be.

[1] Robert Penn Warren, "Traditions, Moral Confusion, the Negro: Themes in Faulkner's," *Bear, Man, & God,* ed. Francis Lee Utley (New York: Random House, 1964), pp. 166–67.

[2] Norman O. Brown, "Introduction," Hesiod's *Theogony* (Indianapolis, IN: Bobbs Merril, 1984), p. 16.

[3] William Faulkner, *The Bear,* in *Bear, Man, & God,* ed. by Francis Lee Utley (New York: Random House, 1964). This text is quoted throughout. *The Bear* appears in Faulkner's collection of stories *Go Down, Moses* but is a work which stands on its own and is usually read as such.

[4] Eugene Ehrlich, *Amo, Amas, Amat and More* (New York: Harper & Row, 1987), p. 39.

[5] Faulkner uses the word "humble" nearly twenty times in this story.

[6] There is an interesting parallel to this image at the end of *Huckleberry Finn.* Just before Huck lights out for the Territory, Tom Sawyer is depicted with "his bullet around his neck on a watch-guard for a watch, and is always seeing what time it is" (p. 245). Tom represents the kind of man Ike would have become without a teacher like Sam Fathers.

[7] Francis Lee Utley, "Pride and Humility: The Cultural Roots of Ike McCaslin," in *Bear, Man, and God,* p. 242.

[8] Martin Buber, *I and Thou,* translated by Ronald Smith (New York: Collier Books, 1958), p. 6.

[9] John Fowles, *The Tree* (New York: Ecco Press, 1979), p. 43.

[10] *Ibid.,* pp. 51–52.

[11] *Ibid.,* pp. 90–91.

[12] In a sexual context that includes white male owners and black women slaves, I think the word rape would be more appropriate here.

[13] R. W. B. Lewis, "The Hero in the New World: William Faulkner's *The Bear,*" in *Bear, Man, and God,* p. 311.

Virginia Woolf's *To the Lighthouse* is about another kind of rejection of feminine wisdom; only in this case the divine feminine is not located in the wilderness, but in Mrs. Ramsay as the archetypal goddess in the guise of the wife and mother.

In his essay "Mythic Patterns in *To the Lighthouse,*" Joseph Blotner argues that Mrs. Ramsay's "attributes are those of major female figures in pagan myth. The most useful myth for interpreting the novel is that of the Primordial Goddess. . . . [Mrs. Ramsay] is a symbol of the female principle in life. Clothed in beauty, an intuitive and fructifying force, she opposes the logical but arid and sterile male principle."[1] The most sustained and tragic irony in the novel is that as striking and powerful as Mrs. Ramsay is as a goddess figure, as generative, fruitful, and healing as her actions and energies are, in terms of her own self-esteem, she is almost invisible to herself. We have so buried and devalued our consciousness of the power of the divine feminine that this consciousness is often barely recognized and appreciated for what it is even by those who still embody it.

Mrs. Ramsay embodies the power of the goddess in the novel; and, while she exercises this power, she doesn't fully realize it, thinking to herself that "she was not good enough to tie [Mr. Ramsay's] shoe strings.[2] Although he needs constant reassurance about his reputation, Mr. Ramsay maintains the highest opinion of himself. However, the novel reveals him to be a pompous, shallow, selfish tyrant as a man, as husband, and as father. In my view, this novel is about the nature of truth and the nature of the consciousness involved in recognizing truth. It presents Mrs. Ramsay and her mystical powers of emotional and intellectual inclusiveness, compassion, and affirmation in sharp contrast to the selfish, narrowly rationalistic obsessions of Mr. Ramsay, the professional philosopher, and his protégé Charles Tansley. *To the Lighthouse* is about two different epistemologies, two very different ways of knowing and being in the world.

Appropriately, the first word of the novel is "Yes," spoken by Mrs. Ramsay. "Yes" is also the first word of the novel's final sentence, spoken by Lily Briscoe, Mrs. Ramsay's devotee and disciple. Mrs. Ramsay is affirming her young son James' desire to travel by boat from their summer residence on the Isle of Skye to the nearby lighthouse. She says: "Yes, of course, if it's fine tomorrow" (p. 9). Mr. Ramsay superimposes his views on hers immediately: "'But,' said his father, stopping in front of the drawing room window, 'it won't be fine'" (p. 10). Mr. Ramsay is described as "standing, as now, lean as a knife, narrow as the blade of one, grinning sarcastically, not only with the pleasure of disillusioning his son and casting ridicule upon his wife . . . but also with some secret conceit at his own accuracy of judgment" (p. 10).

Mr. Ramsay, an academic philosopher, is thought by the sycophant Tansley to be "the greatest metaphysician of the time" (p. 59). Mr. Ramsay's books are described to Lily Briscoe as being about "subject and object and the nature of reality" (p. 38). When Lily doesn't understand what this means, Andrew adds, "'Think of a kitchen table . . . when you're not there'" (p. 38). This is a most revealing image on two counts: first, when Mr. Ramsay is at the table with his gathered family, he doesn't notice them or anything else: "Did he even notice his own daughter's beauty, or whether there was pudding on his plate or roast beef? He would sit at table with them like a person in a dream" (p. 107). Second, when Mrs. Ramsay is at the table, having set it richly with food and drink, she notices and attends to everybody. Symbolic of her own grail-like bounty, she regards the dish of fruit at the table's center and thinks of "a trophy fetched from the bottom of the sea, of Neptune's banquet, of the bunch that hangs with vine leaves over the shoulder of Bacchus . . ." (p. 146).[3] While Mr. Ramsay ponders the nature of reality, like a kitchen table with no one present, Mrs. Ramsay sees to it that the table is abundant with food and is sensitively aware of everyone seated around it. To Mrs. Ramsay, Mr. Ramsay is "born blind, deaf, and dumb to the ordinary things" (p. 107). Tragically, he is "a man afraid to own his own feelings, who could not say, This is what I like—this is what I am" (p. 70).

Mr. Ramsay is preoccupied with his reputation and his standing on the ladder of success relative to other men in his field. As a philosopher, he fancies he is at the letter "Q" in the hierarchical alphabet of thought. To us it may be a silly image, but *he* does not think so:

> He reached Q. Very few people in the whole of England ever
> reached Q. . . . But after Q? What comes next? After Q there are a
> number of letters the last of which is scarcely visible to mortal eyes,
> but glimmers red in the distance. Z is only reached once by one man
> in a generation. Still if he could reach R it would be something. . . .
> He braced himself. He clenched himself. (pp. 53, 54)

Mr. Ramsay understands that there are a very few, "the gifted, the inspired who, miraculously lump all the letters together in one flash—the way of genius" (p. 55). What he doesn't understand is that, in fact, *his wife* is such a gifted, inspired person. However, he will never understand this because, from his point of view, "the folly of women's minds enraged him" (p. 50). But all the while he lives with a woman who possesses "the way of genius" or the consciousness of a mystic:

> She was silent always. She knew then—she knew without having learnt. Her simplicity fathomed what clever people falsified. Her singleness of mind made her drop plumb like a stone, alight exact as a bird, gave her, naturally, this swoop and fall of the spirit upon truth. . . . (p. 46)[4]

Emblematic of the weaver goddess who draws together different strands or threads, Mrs. Ramsay often knits for the lighthouse keeper's little boy "who was threatened with a tuberculous hip" (p. 11). When she sits alone and knits, she has some of her most profound moments of mystical awarenesses when "miraculously . . . all the letters [come] together in one flash.":

> She could be herself, by herself. And that was what now she often felt the need of—to think; well, not even to think. To be silent; to be alone. . . . one shrunk, with a sense of solemnity, to being oneself . . . and this self having shed its attachments was free for the *strangest adventures*. . . . Losing personality, one lost the fret, the hurry, the stir; and there rose to her lips always some exclamation of triumph over life *when things came together* in this peace, this rest, this eternity.
> . . . Often she found herself sitting and looking, sitting and looking, with her work in her hands until she became the thing she looked at—that light for example. . . . It was odd, she thought, how if one was alone, one leant to inanimate things; *trees, streams, flowers;* felt they expressed one; *felt they became one; felt they knew one, in a sense were one;* felt an irrational tenderness thus . . . as for oneself. There rose, and she looked and looked with her needles suspended, there curled up off the floor of the mind, rose from the lake one's being, a mist, a bride to meet her lover. (pp. 95–98; italics mine)

Here is a powerful depiction of a goddess figure in her domestic context if there ever was one. Sitting quietly in her home, knitting, Mrs.

Ramsay recalls the goddess Calypso at her loom or Penelope weaving in her room in Ithaca. She sits unmoving in her chair yet is moved psychically, *transported,* and feels "free for the strangest adventures." There is in her contemplation "the mysterious but indispensable contact with Tao, the hidden 'Mother' of all life and truth."[5] Her becoming one with "trees, streams, flowers" and the "irrational tenderness" she feels for them "as for [her]self" bear a striking resemblance to Buber and Fowles depictions of the I-Thou and "fellow-creature" experience of nature.[6] The last reference in the passage, to that "mist, a bride to meet her lover" reminds us of the mythic *hierosgamos,* or sacred marriage of the self with the otherness of the world.

Ironically, while Mrs. Ramsay embodies such a fecund mythic figure, she has almost no context for properly valuing herself. The power and value of her wisdom are tenuous, quite vulnerable to being completely lost. Were it not for her disciple Lily Briscoe, the whole example of her life might have been lost. This is one way in which we are all vulnerable to the one-sidedness of the patriarchal mind. In Mrs. Ramsay's mind, Mr. Ramsay is the great thinker, even though he is stuck at "Q." (I wonder if Woolf means to imply that Mr. Ramsay can't get to "R" because "R" stands for Reality, that is, the *whole* of reality as Mrs. Ramsay perceives it.)

If we apply Herbert Marcuse's notion that "epistemology is ethics," or that the way we *know* the world powerfully influences the way we *behave* in it;[7] then Mrs. Ramsay's deep, inclusive, ethical way of responding to others grows outs of her inclusive mystical way of embracing the world. She is the one knitting the garment for the tubercular boy. She is the one who feels compassion for the poor and acts on it "when she visited this widow, or that struggling wife in person" (p. 17). She is the one who sees the world's *pain,* its "suffering, death, [and] the poor" (p. 98). Out of that same mystic consciousness which experiences ecstasy in the moment and knows that when reality is encountered this way "It is enough! It is enough!"[8] (p. 100). Mrs. Ramsay also knew "There were eternal problems: suffering; death; the poor. There was always a woman dying of cancer even here" (p. 92). True to the consciousness of the goddess, she has not excluded pain, suffering, or the *dark* side of reality. She knew "There was no treachery too base for the world to commit; she knew that" (p. 98). As she taught what she knew to her children, she taught them to give the same wide embrace to life she did, "And yet she had said to all these children, You shall go through it all" (p. 92).

Lily Briscoe, the young artist who is a guest of the Ramsays, is not one of Mrs. Ramsay's children, but symbolically she is her spiritual daughter. Lily is in a kind of spiritual apprenticeship to Mrs. Ramsay similar to Huck Finn's relationship to Jim or Ike's to Sam Fathers.[9] She sits at Mrs. Ramsay's feet, her arms around the older woman's knees and treasures her life, her example, and her wisdom, wanting to know it for herself:

> She imagined how in the chambers of the mind and heart of the
> woman who was, physically, touching her, were stood, like the
> treasures in the tombs of kings, tablets bearing *sacred inscriptions,*
> which if one could spell them out, would teach one everything . . .
> [but] it was not knowledge but *unity* that she desired, not inscriptions
> on tablets, nothing that could be written in any language known to
> men, but *intimacy itself, which is knowledge,* she had thought, leaning
> her had on Mrs. Ramsay's knee. (p. 79; italics mine)

Perhaps this way of knowing underlies what Mr. Ramsay means when he ridicules women's minds: "He thought, women are always like that; the vagueness of their minds is hopeless. . . . They could not keep anything clearly fixed in their minds" (p. 249).

In striking contrast to Lily and Mrs. Ramsay are Charles Tansley and Mr. Ramsay. The two men are not only blind to Mrs. Ramsay's inner depths and sacred wisdom, they are, in effect, blind to this in all women. Echoing Mr. Ramsay's categorical "the folly of women's minds enraged him" (p. 50) is *his* protégé's misogynist sneer to Lily: "women can't write, women can't paint" (p. 130), which is repeated five times in the book. Mr. Ramsay is a sad figure, a man wholly lacking in contact with his own inner feminine self.

Whereas Mrs. Ramsay is generous and loving, Mr. Ramsay is petty and selfish. His children, especially his son James, hate him for it: "He is a sarcastic brute, James would say. He brings the talk around to himself and his books, James would say. He is intolerably egotistical. Worst of all he is a tyrant" (p. 282). His daughter Cam has similar feelings. Now grown, she recalls "that crass blindness and tyranny of his which had poisoned her childhood . . . so that even now she woke in the night trembling with rage and remembered some command of his, some insolence: 'Do this," 'Do that,' his dominance: his 'Submit to me'" (p. 253).

To the Lighthouse is presented in three sections. The first details the plan to make an outing to a lighthouse off the shore from the Ramsay's summer house. The second section includes World War I, the deaths of two of the Ramsay children (Andrew and Prue), and Mrs. Ramsay's death. In the third section, the remaining family members and Lily Briscoe gather again on the Isle of Skye. Mr. Ramsay, his son James, and his daughter Cam finally make the trip to the lighthouse. But it is too little, too late. Clearly, Mr. Ramsay must undertake many spiritual journeys if he is to transform all the years of deprecating his family, dominating them emotionally, and "the pleasure of disillusioning his son" (p. 10). When they finally do arrive at the lighthouse, Mr. Ramsay turns to his son and says, "Well done!" (p. 306) Mr. Ramsay has finally offered a word of praise to his son, but what a niggardly, miniscule compliment it is. James has endured a lifetime of emotional starvation at the hands of his father, so to him this stock English phrase means a great deal: "He was so pleased that he was not going to let anybody share a grain of his pleasure. His father had praised him" (p. 306).

To the reader, the praise bestowed on James is pathetically minimal, but to James, each tiny grain means *everything*. Immediately after hearing these two words of praise, both James and Cam experience a sudden opening of warmth and empathy for their father. Like any two emotionally starved children, "They watched him, both of them . . . what do you want? They both wanted to ask. Ask us anything and we will give it to you. But he did not ask them anything. He sat and looked at the island and he might be thinking, We perished, each alone, or he might be thinking, I have reached it. I have found it; but he said nothing" (p. 308). The novel ends two pages later. Has Mr. Ramsay actually changed? If he has started to move away from his emotional sterility and his selfishness, the movement is so miniscule as to be only a beginning. As Lily says, "He seemed to her a figure of infinite pathos. . . . There was no helping Mr. Ramsay on the journey he was going" (p. 230).

Lily, on the other hand, has traveled far and learned much from Mrs. Ramsay, her spiritual guide. In spite of Tansley, she continues to paint. Towards the end of the novel, she senses the presence of Mrs.

Ramsay while she works on a painting involving a tree.[10] "One wanted, she thought, dipping her brush deliberately, to be on a level with ordinary experience to feel simply that's a chair, that's a table, and yet at the same time, It's a miracle, it's an ecstasy" (p. 300)—words Mrs. Ramsay would have thought herself. Lily makes a brushstroke in the center of her canvas and the novel ends with these lines: "It was done; it was finished. Yes, she thought, laying down her brush in extreme fatigue, I have had my vision" (p. 310).

Sitting at her feet, and at her bountiful table, Lily has learned much from the goddess in Mrs. Ramsay. What she learned has become part of her own vision as a woman and artist.

Personal Commentary

Mr. Ramsay is an academic philosopher who has published several books and has a modest reputation in his field. Like Willy Loman, what success he achieves does not include his relationship to the feminine, his feelings, a sense of compassion or his connection with his children. But in my mind, Mr. Ramsay is more culpable than Willy Loman because he is married to a woman who *embodies* everything he lacks, yet he remains oblivious, both to her wisdom and his own need for it. His one-dimensional patriarchal world view is passed on from father to son.

When the little boating party arrives at the lighthouse, Mr. Ramsay finally does compliment James. James and Cam eagerly await some other morsel of response from their father, but he says nothing to them. It is hard for men who are not as locked away inside their emotions as much as Mr. Ramsay to comprehend his silence and his *relational nothingness*. The truly tragic thing that I've observed is that such a silence is usually not a *deliberate* withholding. It's not that Mr. Ramsay (or men like him) have a lot to say or ask, but choose not to interact. Mr. Ramsay and his ilk simply don't *have anything at all to say to their children,* unless those children want to talk about his philosophy or business. They don't know how to talk with their children because they can't *be* fellow human beings with them. A man who doesn't know what he feels can't experience compassion, or what John Fowles calls "fellow-feeling." In his emphasis on a rigid rationality, Mr. Ramsay has so abstracted himself from everyone, including whole dimensions of himself, that he is *stunted* by his own inner emptiness.

There was a time when I was in grave danger of becoming a Mr. Ramsay. I was a philosophy major in college and went on to study philosophy in graduate school. I certainly can't blame philosophy for what happened to me. What I can say is that philosophy's emphasis on logic, rationality, consistency, and the kinds of abstractions Mr. Ramsay ponders were not *helping me* to know myself. At the time I needed to know myself and be more *embodied* in my thinking and feeling. Had I read this novel then, I'd have thought of Mr. Ramsay as idiosyncratic and temperamental, perhaps as a man with difficult parental characteristics. But all these things would have seemed quite permissible to me then because he was, after all, a father and a "great thinker." Now I see him in a quite different light.

I feel great sadness for him because I know he will eventually lose his children—as people, friends, and life companions. One's children are forever, and fortunate parents are the ones for whom this fact is a treasure, not a source of pain. Mr. Ramsay angers me now; I can't help thinking that in being married to Mrs. Ramsay, he might at least have learned *some* of her generosity, *some* of her emotional self-extension and good will. For fathers to achieve a lifelong authentic connection with their children, they often must be able to relinquish the *distance* men are taught to keep between themselves and others. This means being able to learn what Lily has learned from Mrs. Ramsay: to desire contact. Unity with our children and other people and intimacy are forms of knowledge just as important (if not more so) than philosophical knowledge. It is painful to recognize that Mr. Ramsay the great thinker, the man of great knowledge, knows all that he does but doesn't know himself or his own children.

[1] Joseph L. Blotner, "Mythic Patterns in *To the Lighthouse*," *PMLA* 71, Sept. 1956, pp. 547, 549.

[2] Virginia Woolf, *To the Lighthouse* (New York: Harcourt Brace & World, 1955), p. 51. This is the text quoted throughout.

[3] We have encountered references to trophies throughout this book, from Gilgamesh's quest for the flower of immortality at the bottom of the sea, to Biff's football trophy valued so highly by his father, Willy Loman, to Tom Sawyer's bullet/watch-fob, to Sir Gawain's green girdle, and Old Ben, the bear. That Mrs. Ramsay would regard an ordinary bowl of fruit in a such a mythic light reveals how able she is to see the ordinary domestic world in sacred terms, and at the same time not feel she must possess it as a trophy.

[4] The reader may recall here an early comment from Nor Hall on "the essential

value of silence in feminine mysteries." *The Moon and the Virgin* (New York: Harper and Row, 1980), p. 59.

⁵ Thomas Merton, *The Way of Chuang Tzu* (New York: New Directions, 1969), p. 26.

⁶ See Chapter Nine, pp. 122–131.

⁷ Herbert Marcuse, *One-Dimensional Man* (Boston: Beacon Press, 1966), p. 125.

⁸ This line always reminds me of the first stanza of Emily Dickinson's poem #677 in the Thomas Johnson *Complete Poems* (Boston: Little Brown, 1960), p. 335:

> To be alive—is Power—
> Existence—in itself—
> Without a further function—
> Omnipotence—Enough—

⁹ Lily's name suggests some vegetation spirit; it is drawn from the natural world of plants, as is Huck's. The lily is also a symbol of the virgin goddess.

¹⁰ The great Goddess is frequently compared to a tree or associated with trees, and Mrs. Ramsay herself is compared to one: "she grew still like a tree which has been tossing and quivering and now, when the breeze falls, settles, leaf by leaf, into quiet" (p. 177).

Conclusion

Unlike an act of intellect that can swiftly register facts, analyze, or classify them, the feminine quality of understanding conceives a content, walks around it, participates affectively in it, and then brings it forth into the world.

—*Ann Ulanov*

The Labyrinth is one of the oldest of symbols; it depicts the way to the unknown center, the mystery of death and rebirth, the risk of the search, the danger of losing the way, the quest, the finding and the ability to return. . . . Perhaps what matters is not so much the reaching of a goal but the conscious journey on the labyrinthine path.

—*Edward Whitmont*

Much as I have respect and admiration for his poetry, I must disagree quite pointedly with the central assumptions of Paul Zweig's provocative book, *The Adventurer: The Fate of Adventure in the Western World.* In fact, I view my work as a counterargument to his main thesis. His thesis reflects a prevalent way of viewing many Western classics. Writing about Gilgamesh, Odysseus, Sir Gawain, and other male adventurers in Western literature, Zweig says:

The adventurer, in his desire to reinvent himself as a man, reinvents his emotions, so that they may be served *wholly* by *male pleasures:* the rooted society of women *superseded* by the mobile society of men. . . . The adventurer represents a poignant male fantasy: moved by his desire to *vanquish* the many faces of woman, he reinvents the shape of manhood itself so as *to free it* from its multiple attachments to the feminine.[1]

141

In this discussion I have espoused the view that Gilgamesh, Willy Loman, Odysseus, Huck, and the other characters are struggling with a kind of self-invention that *includes* the face of women and that would *discover* the face of the woman inside them, a face that belongs to the mythic feminine.

Zweig maintains that underlying "the unrelenting masculinity of adventure literature" is the fact that "the adventurer is in flight from women. Because he cannot cope with the erotic and social hegemony of women,[2] he flees them even into death" (p. 61). "The adventurer's essential triumph is masculine. His gift is to bind the binder, to outwit and *defeat* the mysterious identities of woman" (p. 69).

The men in these stories (and women like Lily Briscoe) are struggling to make contact with a kind of consciousness that lies buried and negated in a patriarchal culture.

The real adventure we face today has to do with survival: saving ourselves and our planet and rescuing the lost feminine spirit in ourselves. The patriarchal world view that *real* men seek to defeat "the mysterious identities of women," to "vanquish the many faces of woman," or desire fulfillment through being "served wholly by male pleasures" denies the great force of the feminine qualities of understanding and connectedness that we need in order to restore a sense of balance.

To say that the stories discussed here *support* this world view is in my mind a fundamental misreading of their intent. Rather, I suggest that many of the classic "adventure stories" recognize the imbalance of our patriarchal culture and describe the efforts of men who try, with varying degrees of success, to become whole by developing the feminine in themselves.

Yeats wrote, "Why should we honor those that die upon the field of battle, a man may show as reckless a courage in entering into the abyss of himself."[3] The real adventure is the interior one, the one into the labyrinthine underworld that exists inside us. For many, that interior world includes the face of the Goddess as our feminine side. As Starhawk notes:

> For a man, the Goddess, as well as being the universal life force, is his own, hidden, female self. She embodies all the qualities society teaches him *not* to recognize in himself. His first experience of Her may therefore seem somewhat stereotyped; She will be the cosmic

lover, the gentle nurturer, the eternally desired Other, the Muse, all
that he is not. As he becomes more whole and becomes aware of his
own 'female' qualities, She seems to change, to show him a new face,
always holding up the mirror that shows what to him is still
ungraspable. He may chase Her forever, and She will elude him, but
through the attempt he will grow, until he too learns to find Her
within.[4]

It is important to note that this view of men and the feminine empha-
sizes plurality ("as he . . . becomes aware of his own 'female' qualities"), change ("she seems to change, to show him a new face"), and the
lifelong nature of this endeavor ("He may chase her forever").

I can identify with the male figures in these ten great stories in
many different ways. I'm certainly no authority on the feminine, and I
don't pretend to be whole. I'm simply a man on a long journey toward
recovering the sacred feminine in my life. I'm indebted to Mark Van
Doren for helping me begin the journey, and to many writers who af-
forded me useful insights about the feminine principle. Robert Bly has
been an important resource for me in both the power of his poems and
the courage and personal candor of his prose. Men need to not just
know about the feminine but to find ways to experience it and practice
it in our lives. Again, plurality, change, and the long view are needed
for understanding. There is no one view of the feminine, no *single* way;
it is a lifelong commitment.

For me one of the most important ways of practicing the presence
of the sacred feminine has to do with the *power of listening:* listening to
the body, which Ivan Ilyich is fatally slow to do; listening to Nature,
which Huck Finn and Ike McCaslin learn to do with life-changing consequences; listening to the voices of the inner self, which Willy Loman
begins to do too late in his life; listening to the signs, dreams, and chance
occurrences, which Bottom knows how to do respectfully and Macbeth
does not. Above all, we must listen to the voices of the women and men
in our lives. Their voices are able to instruct us in the feminine through
teaching, writing, and example.

In order to listen, we must find ways to slow down long enough to
be able to hear and to pay attention to what we hear. We must fully
receive these communications, whether they are ambiguous, many-sided,
or shiningly clear. In the commentary accompanying the beautiful pho-

tographs of prehistoric standing stones, stone circles, and dolmen in Paul Caponigro's *Megaliths*, he writes:

> Not wanting to lose the thread of something I could scarcely take hold of, I learned to be at the sites not merely to take pictures, but to give myself over to the total experience as best I knew how. Meaning hung in the air about the stones, and I had to gather concentration and quiet within myself to even begin conversing with these earth ambassadors, whose silence and sense of centeredness were sobering and internally cleansing to me. I felt this mysterious earth energy to be in greater concentration where the stones were placed. I watched and waited, and quietly worked the camera while trying to penetrate the unseen. I would continue this process until my mind quieted and my emotions blended with the timelessness. . . . Impressions I received in the presence of the stones opened gateways that led me to a profound sense of harmony.[5]

Clearly he is a man who knows a great deal about the art of listening as a way of receiving. Marija Gimbutas' says in *The Language of the Goddess* that these kinds of megaliths may be thought of as "an extension of the centrally concentrated Goddess energy."[6] So we might say that Caponigro is writing about listening to and *communing with* the earth as a voice of the sacred feminine. I would add that in these actions he is performing the work of the Green Man. It is the work we all do when we recognize the false sense of duality between nature and our inner selves and realize that the world of nature also exists within us.

In my own life, writing poetry and meditation have been important practices because they have taught me the discipline of letting go and being receptive. Meditation allows me to simply receive my life, breath by breath. I have found that my way into a poem often involves first receiving the Muse's offerings and then working with them, to shape and edit what has been received. I understand and experience the sacred feminine at this time in my life as a way of being patient and, rather than forcing things, letting them ripen. Ann Ulanov says it well when she writes that the feminine "is a way of submitting to a process, which is seen as simply happening and is not to be forced or achieved by an effort of the will. The quality of feminine activity is a mixture of attentiveness and contemplation."[7] The paradox is that one must *will* this way of activity until it becomes second nature. The sacred feminine in this sense is a kind of discipline. In my life, I must first make time to meditate and then wait for and write the poems.

This may not be how other men come to know the sacred feminine. Each of us will experience a different changing, multifaceted relationship with such a force in ourselves and in our world. What is crucial is that we come to share a common assumption about the importance of the sacred feminine in our lives. If we shared this common assumption, we would be less alone and isolated from one another. Joseph Campbell writes:

> Furthermore, we have not even to risk the adventure alone, for the heroes of all time have gone before us. The labyrinth is thoroughly known. We have only to follow the thread of the hero path, and where we had thought to find an abomination, we shall find a god. And where we had thought to slay another, we shall slay ourselves. Where we had thought to travel outward, we will come to the center of our own existence. And where we had thought to be alone, we will be with all the world.[8]

A work of literature is very much like a labyrinth; it offers the reader examples of others who have gone on the adventure before. Great works may help teach us about both the wondrous and terrible contents of our heritage and show us ways we might transform ourselves to experience our own rebirth. Joseph Campbell may be right, but I would say that when we come to the *real* center of our lives, we shall find not only a god but a goddess as well.

[1] Paul Zweig, *The Adventurer: The Fate of Adventure in the Western World* (New York: Basic Books, Inc., 1974), pp. 75; 79. Italics mine.

[2] In a patriarchal world one wonders how substantial that "hegemony" really is.

[3] Quoted by Richard Ellmann, in *Yeats: The Man and the Masks* (New York: W.W. Norton, 1978), p. 6.

[4] Starhawk, *The Spiral Dance: A Rebirth of the Ancient Religion of the Great Goddess* (New York: Harper & Row, 1979), p. 85.

[5] Paul Caponigro, *Megaliths* (New York: Little Brown, 1986).

[6] Marija Gimbutas, T*he Language of the Goddess* (New York: Harper & Row, 1989), p. 311.

[7] Ann Belford Ulanov, *The Feminine* (Evanston, IL: Northwestern University Press, 1971), p. 173.

[8] Joseph Campbell, *The Power of Myth* (New York: Doubleday, 1988), p. 123.

Bibliography

Epigraphs:

Page vii: Carol Christ. *Laughter of Aphrodite.* San Francisco: Harper & Row, 1987, p. 111.

Robert Bly. *Sleepers Joining Hands.* New York: Harper & Row, 1985, p. 34.

Introduction: John Fowles, Interview, *The Paris Review,* Summer, 1989, p. 60.

Chapter 1: *Gilgamesh.* Translated and edited by John Gardner and John Maier. New York: Alfred A. Knopf, 1984, p. 22.

Chapter 2: Arthur Miller. *Timebends: A Life.* New York: Grove Press, 1987, p. 337.

William Butler Yeats. Quoted in *Yeats: The Man and the Masks.* Richard Ellmann. New York: W.W. Norton, 1987, p. 6.

Chapter 3: Mircea Eliade. *Myths, Dreams and Mysteries.* New York: Harper & Row, 1975, p. 174.

Chapter 4: Mark Twain. Quoted in *Mark Twain and His World.* Justin Kaplan. New York: Simon and Schuster, p. 166.

Chapter 5: Albert Einstein. *What I Believe.* Edited by Mark Booth. New York: Crossroad, 1984, p. 27.

Chapter 6: Michel de Montaigne. "Of Repenting." *Essays.* Translated by Donald Frame. Princeton: Van Nostrand Co., 1943, p. 177.

Chapter 7: Starhawk. *Womanspirit Rising.* Edited by Carol Christ and Judith Plaskow. San Francisco: Harper & Row, 1979, p. 263.

Chapter 8: Pam Wright. "Living With Death As a Teacher." *Woman of Power.* 8 (Winter 1988), p. 12.

Chapter 9: D. H. Lawrence. *Sex, Literature, and Censorship.* New York: Viking, 1959, p. 106.

Chapter 10: Edward Whitmont. *Return of the Goddess.* New York: Crossroad. 1982, p. 86.

Conclusion: Ann Belford Ulanov. *The Feminine.* Evanston: Northwestern University Press, 1971, p. 171.

Edward Whitmont. *The Symbolic Quest.* Princeton: Princeton University Press, 1969, p. 306.

References:

Anonymous. *The Epic of Gilgamesh.* Translated by N. K. Sandars. New York: Penguin, 1981.

Anonymous. *Gilgamesh.* Translated by John Gardner and John Maier. New York: Alfred A. Knopf, 1984.

Anonymous. *Sir Gawain and the Green Knight.* Translated by Brian Stone. Baltimore: Penguin, 1964.

Berry, Wendell. *The Unsettling of America: Culture and Agriculture.* San Francisco: Sierra Club Books, 1978.

Blake, William. *The Essential Blake.* Edited by Stanley Kunitz. New York: Ecco Press, 1983.

Blotner, Joseph L., "Mythic Patterns" in *To the Lighthouse, Publication of Modern Languages,* 71 (Sept. 1956).

Bly, Robert. *Sleepers Joining Hands.* New York: Harper and Row, 1974.

_____. *Talking All Morning.* Ann Arbor: University of Michigan Press, 1980.

Bolen, Jean Shinoda. "The Feminine Emerging," *Yoga Journal* (Jan./Feb. 1988).

Briggs, Katherine. *Pale Hecate's Team: An Examination of the Beliefs on Witchcraft and Magic Among Shakespeare's Contemporaries and His Immediate Successors,* New York: The Humanities Press, 1962.

Brooks, Cleanth. *The Well Wrought Urn.* New York: Harcourt Brace & Co., 1947.

Brown, Norman O. "Introduction." Hesiod's *Theogony.* Indianapolis: Bobbs-Merrill Co., 1984.

_____. "Daphne, or Metamorphosis." *Myths, Dreams, and Religion.* Edited by Joseph Campbell. New York: E.P. Dutton, 1970.

Buber, Martin. *I and Thou.* Translated by Walter Kaufmann. New York: Charles Scribner's Sons, 1970.

_____. *I and Thou.* Translated by Ronald Smith. New York: Collier Books, 1958.

Burkhardt, Titus. "The Return of Ulysses." *Parabola,* 3 (Nov. 1978).

Christ, Carol. *Laughter of Aphrodite: Reflection on a Journey to the Goddess.* San Francisco: Harper & Row, 1987.

Cirlot, J. E. *A Dictionary of Symbols.* New York: Philosophical Library, 1962.

Campbell, Joseph. Foreword to *The Language of the Goddess,* by Marija Gimbutas. San Francisco: Harper & Row, 1989.

_____. *The Masks of God: Occidental Mythology.* New York: Penguin, 1986.

_____. *The Hero With a Thousand Faces.* Princeton: Princeton University Press, 1973.

_____. *The Power of Myth.* New York: Doubleday, 1988.

Caponigro, Paul. *Megaliths.* New York: Little Brown & Co., 1986.

Cavendish, Richard. *The Black Arts.* New York: Capricorn Books, 1968.

Dickinson, Emily. *Complete Poems.* Edited by Thomas Johnson. Boston: Little Brown, 1960.

Doran, Madeleine. Introduction to *A Midsummer Night's Dream,* by William Shakespeare. Baltimore: Penguin, 1967.

Ehrlich, Eugene. *Amo, Amas, Amat and More.* New York: Harper & Row, 1987.

Eisler, Riane. *The Chalice and the Blade.* San Francisco: Harper & Row, 1987.

Eliade, Mircea. *Myths, Dreams, and Mysteries.* New York: Harper Torchbooks, 1975.

_____. *Cosmos and History: The Myth of the Eternal Return.* New York: Harper Torchbooks, 1959.

_____. *The Sacred and the Profane.* New York: Harcourt, Brace and World, 1959.

_____. Editor. *The Encyclopedia of Religion.* New York: MacMillan, 1983.

Eliot, T.S. "Introduction." *Adventures of Huckleberry Finn, A Norton Critical Edition.* New York: W.W. Norton, 1962.

Ellmann, Richard. *Yeats: The Man and the Masks.* New York: W.W. Norton, 1978.

Faulkner, William. *The Bear. Bear, Man and God.* Edited by Francis Lee Utley, et.al. New York: Random House, 1964.

Fowles, John. *The Tree.* New York: Ecco Press, 1979.

_____. Interview. *The Paris Review.* (Summer 1989): 40-63.

Fox, Matthew. *The Coming of the Cosmic Christ.* San Francisco: Harper & Row, 1988.

French, Marilyn. *Shakespeare's Division of Experience.* London: Jonathan Cape, 1982.

Gimbutas, Marija. *The Goddesses and Gods of Old Europe.* Berkeley: University of California Press, 1982.

_____. *The Language of the Goddess.* San Francisco: Harper & Row, 1989.

Hall, Nor. *The Moon and the Virgin: Reflections on the Archetypal Feminine.* New York: Harper & Row, 1980.

Harding, M. Esther. *Woman's Mysteries, Ancient and Modern.* New York: Harper & Row, 1971.

Hawkes, J. *Dawn of the Gods.* London, 1968.

Hoffman, Daniel G. "Black Magic–and White–in *Huckleberry Finn.*" *Adventures of Huckleberry Finn, A Norton Critical Edition.* New York: W.W. Norton, 1962.

Homer. *The Odyssey.* Translated by Robert Fitzgerald. New York: Anchor Books, 1963.

Johnson, Ronald. *The Book of the Green Man.* New York: W.W. Norton, 1967.

Jung, C.G. *Aspects of the Feminine.* Princeton: Princeton University Press, 1982.

Kramer, Samuel Noah. *From the Poetry of Sumer.* Berkeley: University of California Press, 1979.

Lerner, Gerda. *The Creation of Patriarchy.* New York: Oxford University Press, 1986.

Lewis, C.S. *The Discarded Image: An Introduction to Medieval and Renaissance Literature.* Cambridge: Cambridge University Press, 1964.

Lewis, R.W.B. "The Hero in the New World: William Faulkner's *The Bear.*" *Bear, Man, and God.* New York: Random House, 1964.

Lynn, Kenneth S. "You Can't Go Home Again." *Adventures of Huckleberry Finn, A Norton Critical Edition.* New York: W.W. Norton, 1962.

Marcuse, Herbert. *One-Dimensional Man.* Boston: Beacon Press, 1966.

McKee, Char. "Feminism: A Vision of Love." *The Goddess Re-Awakening.* Edited by Shirley Nicholson. Wheaton: Theosophical Publishing House, 1989.

Merton, Thomas. *The Way of Chuang Tzu.* New York: New Directions, 1969.

Miller, Arthur. *Death of a Salesman.* New York: Viking, 1960.

_____. *Timebends: A Life.* New York: Grove Press, 1987.

Murray, Gilbert. *Five Stages of Greek Religion.* Garden City: Doubleday, 1955.

Neumann, Erich. *The Great Mother: An Analysis of the Archetype.* Princeton: Princeton University Press, 1974.

_____. "On the Moon and Matriarchal Consciousness." *Dynamic Aspects of the Psyche.* New York: The Analytical Psychology Club, 1956.

Olson, Carl. Editor. *The Book of the Goddess: Past and Present.* New York: Crossroad Press, 1986.

Otto, Rudolph. *The Idea of the Holy.* New York: Oxford University Press, 1980.

Perera, Sylvia. *The Descent to the Goddess.* Toronto: Inner City Books, 1981.

Plato. *The Portable Plato.* Translated by Benjamin Jowett. New York: Viking, 1965.

Rabuzzi, Kathryn Allen. *Motherself: A Mythic Analysis of Motherhood.* Bloomington: Indiana University Press, 1988.

_____. *The Sacred and the Feminine.* New York: Seabury Press, 1982.

Raffel, Burton. "Introduction." *Sir Gawain and the Green Knight.* New York: New American Library, 1970.

Reuther, Rosemary. "Motherearth and the Megamachine: A Theology of Liberation in a Feminine, Somatic and Ecological Perspective." *Womanspirit Rising.* Edited by Carol Christ and Juith Plaskow. San Francisco: Harper & Row, 1979.

Russell, Jeffrey Burton. *Witchcraft in the Middle Ages.* Ithaca: Cornell University Press. 1972.

Sewall, Elizabeth. *The Orphic Voice.* New Haven: Yale University Press, 1960.

Sexson, Lynda. *Ordinarily Sacred.* New York: Crossroad, 1982.

Shakespeare, William. *A Midsummer Night's Dream.* Baltimore: Penguin Books, 1967.

_____. *The Tragedy of Macbeth.* Edited by Alfred Harbage. Baltimore: Penguin Books, 1956.

_____. *The Riverside Shakespeare.* Edited by G. Blakemore Evans. Boston: Houghton Mifflin Co., 1974.

Spence, Lewis. *British Fairy Origins.* Wellingborough, U.K: The Aquarian Press, 1946.

Spencer, Theodore. *Shakespeare and the Nature of Man.* New York: Collier Books, 1966.

Starhawk. *The Spiral Dance: A Rebirth of the Ancient Religion of the Great Goddess.* San Francisco: Harper & Row, 1979.

Steiner, George. Editor. *Homer: A Collection of Critical Essays.* Englewood Cliffs: Prentice Hall, 1962.

Stone, Merlin. *Ancient Mirrors of Womanhood.* Boston: Beacon Press, 1984.

_____. "Endings and Origins." *Woman of Power.* 8 (Winter 1988).

_____. "Introduction." *The Goddess Re-Awakening.* Edited by Shirley Nicholson. Wheaton: Theosophical Publishing House, 1989.

Tillyard, E.M.W. *The Elizabethan World Picture.* New York: Vintage Books, n.d.

Tolstoy, Leo. *The Death of Ivan Ilyich.* Translated by Lynn Solotaroff. New York: Bantam Books, 1987.

Twain, Mark. *Adventures of Huckleberry Finn.* Boston: Houghton Mifflin, 1958.

_____. *Adventures of Huckleberry Finn, A Norton Critical Edition.* New York: W.W. Norton, 1962.

_____. *The Adventures of Tom Sawyer.* Avon, Connecticut: The Heritage Press, 1964.

_____. *Life on the Mississippi.* New York: New American Library, 1961.

Ulanov, Ann Belford. *The Feminine: In Jungian Psychology and Christian Theology.* Evanston: Northwestern University Press, 1971.

_____. *Religion and the Unconscious.* Philadelphia: The Westminister Press, 1975.

Utley, Francis Lee. "Pride and Humility: The Cultural Roots of Ike McCaslin." *Bear, Man, and God.* New York: Random House, 1964.

Van Doren, Mark. *Liberal Education.* Boston: Beacon Hill, 1962.

Walker, Barbara G. *The Woman's Encyclopedia of Myths and Secrets.* San Francisco: Harper & Row, 1963.

Warren, Robert Penn. "Tradition, Moral Confusion, the Negro: Themes in Faulkner's Work." *Bear, Man, and God.* New York: Random House, 1964.

Weil, Simone. *"The Iliad,* or The Poem of Force." Wallingford, Pa.: Pendle Hill, 1981.

Weiss, Theodore. *The Berath of Clowns and Kings: Shakespeare's Early Comedies and Histories.* New York: Atheneum, 1971.

Whitmont, Edward. *Return of the Goddess.* New York: Crossroad, 1982.

Woodman, Marion. *Addiction to Perfection.* Toronto: Inner City Books, 1982.

Woolf, Virginia. *To the Lighthouse.* New York: Harcourt Brace and World, 1955.

Wright, Pam. "Living with Death as a Teacher." *Woman of Power.* 8 (Winter 1988).

Zweig, Paul. *The Adventurer: The Fate of Adventure in the Western World.* New York: Basic Books, 1974.

Index

Other Titles for Further Reading in the Goddess Tradition

WOMEN OF THE CELTS

Jean Markale
ISBN 0-89281-150-1
315 pages, 6 x 9
$12.95 paperback

Journey deep into the mythic world of the Celts, where both men and women become whole by realizing the feminine principle in its entirety. The Celts, who at one time were spread throughout Europe, left permanent traces of a culture in which women were the spiritual and moral pivot. Through legends and literature, *Women of the Celts* reveals the impact of this heritage on modern attitudes toward marriage, sexual liberation, and love, and shows the Celtic woman to be an enduring symbol of human freedom.

EARTH HONORING

The New Male Sexuality
Robert Lawlor
ISBN 0-89281-254-0
224 pages, 6 x 9
$16.95 hardcover
ISBN 0-89281-428-4
$12.95 paperback

"Lawlor focuses his attention on the disastrous consequences of our Western misappropriation of male sexual energy. He draws from the teachings of Taoist, Tantric, and tribal culture ritualism to draft possible roadmaps for men to move into an intelligent, compassionate, and ecstatic appreciation of their life-force energies...his larger vision encompasses the planet." —**EastWest Journal**

EROS AND THE MYSTERIES OF LOVE

The Metaphysics of Sex
Julius Evola
ISBN 0-89281-315-6
384 pages, 6 x 9
$12.95 paperback

Religion, mysticism, folklore, and mythology all contain erotic forms in which the deeper possibilities of the human sexual experience are recognized. In this perceptive study of sexual energies, Evola shows how eroticism can lead to a displacement of the boundaries of the ego and the emergence of profound states of consciousness.

"(Evola) uses the bow, hitting his target with consummate accuracy and illuminating in a few words a whole area of thought hitherto unrecognized by most of us." —**Gnosis Magazine**

KALI

The Feminine Force
Ajit Mookerjee
ISBN 0-89281-212-5
112 pages, 7 x 10
104 illustrations, 18 in full color
$12.95 paperback

According to Hindu tradition, we are living in the age of Kali, a time of resurgence of the divine feminine spirit. The author draws on the powerful imagery of painting, sculpture, and literature in this celebration of Kali and the rich meanings of the goddess in her many forms.

"The many images in this volume convey better than words what this deity means to the Hindus. However, Mookerjee's illuminating commentary...brings out the universal content of the Kali image to which, if we will allow it, we are likely to find archetypal resonances within us." —**Spectrum Review**

KUNDALINI

The Arousal of the Inner Energy
Ajit Mookerjee
ISBN 0-89281-020-3
112 pages 7 x 10
61 illustrations, 16 in full color
$12.95 paperback

Beautifully illustrated with classical Indian art, this companion volume to *Kali* details the Kundalini experience from the modern perspective, drawing on both Eastern and Western accounts.

These and other Inner Traditions titles are available at many fine bookstores or, to order direct, send a check or money order for the total amount, payable to Inner Traditions, plus $2.00 shipping and handling for the first book and $1.00 for each additional book to:

AIDC/Inner Traditions
64 Depot Road
Colchester, VT 05446

Or call toll-free
1-800-445-6638 (outside Vermont)
878-0315 (within Vermont)

Be sure to request a free catalog.